KU-060-725

THE BOUNTY MAN

Bounty hunter M'Grea is a big man, topping most of his fellows by several inches, and can hold his own with the best in a fight with fists — or guns. Now he has killers Dutch George and King Rattler in his hands — all that remains is to turn them in and collect the bounties. But that isn't going to be easy: dangerous Apaches are very near, and the trio is about to walk into a deadly trap . . .

*Books by Gordon Landsborough
in the Linford Western Library:*

THE BANDAGED RIDERS
UNION SOLDIER
IRON JACK RIDES

GORDON LANDSBOROUGH

THE BOUNTY MAN

Complete and Unabridged

LINFORD
Leicester

First published in Great Britain in 1953
as
The Bounty Man
by Mike M'Cracken

First Linford Edition
published 2016

Copyright © 1953, 2003
by Gordon Landsborough
All rights reserved

A catalogue record for this book is available
from the British Library.

ISBN 978-1-4448-3007-1

Published by
F. A. Thorpe (Publishing)
Anstey, Leicestershire

Set by Words & Graphics Ltd.
Anstey, Leicestershire
Printed and bound in Great Britain by
T. J. International Ltd., Padstow, Cornwall

This book is printed on acid-free paper

1

King Rattler

They were Apaches. Big M'Grea knew that the moment he set eyes on them. Only Apaches of all Indian tribes so far south used dogs to transport their belongings.

There were a lot of them, too. Eyes just showing above the natural barricade of boulders, Big M'Grea made a rough estimate of the long, hurrying, snaky file that wound up the arid, scrub-covered gulch that gave out finally on to the vast Staked Plains of far-west Texas.

'Two hundred,' he murmured to himself. His eyes were slits against the fierce noonday sun, almost closed and yet missing nothing.

There was a Sharp's rifle in his massive, weather-browned hands — so

1

big they made it look like a toy. But that rifle was pointing not at the approaching Indians but at the sullen, hating men who stood ten paces away, holding the heads of their horses to prevent them from whinnying and betraying them to their Indian enemies. And Big M'Grea wasn't missing a move from either of them; for the moment they were to him much more dangerous than the Apaches half a mile away.

Dutch George, big and loose and shambling, was a killer who would kill M'Grea as soon as look at him, given the chance, and M'Grea knew it. And King Rattler, Dutch George's companion in crime, was level with him in any evil he would do.

Which was why the big, shrewd cowboy had hobbled the two men when they saw the distant advancing cloud of dust — hobbled them and not the horses! He wasn't giving the gunmen chance to ride off while he lay sizing up the new danger ahead of them.

M'Grea was big. In a land of big men

he topped most by several inches. It wasn't too good, that size, when it came to riding, because unless he had a horse to match his build they quickly foundered. But a man doesn't ride all day always. Sometimes he gets into fights, and then height and weight are an asset.

M'Grea, anyway, carried most of his weight where it should be packed — above the waistline. Below his waist he had the long, lean legs of a man who didn't build muscle by a lot of walking, for men who live a lot in the saddle don't grow big down below. But his shoulders were mighty — even massive; and his arms were as thick as five-year-old cottonwoods, and just as tough.

Wrestling with antagonistic beef out on the range as well as at rodeos had given him that top weight and a strength to match, and when it came to a fight, with men or beasts, Big M'Grea could hold his own. Dutch George and King Rattler knew it — knew it very well by now — but knowledge had come a bit too late to them.

They watched with glittering malevolent eyes as he sprawled a bit above them on the rocky knoll that gave men and horses cover.

He was no show-off puncher, this big M'Grea. He didn't go in for silver bridle rings and Mexican leatherwork on his saddle. He was no dude with fancy boots and fancier spurs, and his Colt guns were plain and unornamented, unlike so many other cowboys.

He was a big, careless man in his dress. Just now he wore a shirt that had been blue until the fierce sun bleached most of the colour out of it; he wore an old vest that was permanently open because it couldn't quite meet across his front. And soiled, torn jeans completed his attire — jeans that were comfortable on him because they didn't fit closely to his large limbs, like those fancy riding pants that brought on the sweat and kept you slipping in the saddle after a couple of hours' riding.

One leg of the jeans was tucked into his riding boot; the other had worked its way out and hung outside. Big M'Grea didn't give a damn. It felt comfortable.

Lines deepened as his brows puckered together. He couldn't make this out. He knew Indians — he'd fought against them as a kid clinging to the tailboard of their prairie schooner when they'd come West to make new land, him and his family. They'd killed his father with an arrow wound in the arm. It hadn't looked much of a sore at first, but that arrowhead had been dug into dirt before firing, and the dirt had carried infection, as the Indian had known it would, and brave pioneer Lem M'Grea had died as surely as if that arrow had pierced his heart and not his fleshy forearm.

Twice Indians had devastated the family holding and butchered many of the neighbouring settlers, and each time young M'Grea had taken to horse in fierce, vengeful pursuit, and with a posse of bitter settlers had carried the war back into Indian country. Once he'd even been an Indian prisoner, but he didn't like to think of that time. They'd had him for a couple of days, but then help had ridden through the Indian lines and picked him up. He'd been fifteen at the time.

Yes, Big Tom M'Grea knew Indians all right.

Now he was puzzled, knowing what he did about his natural enemy.

This column consisted mostly of squaws and papooses. In all, there were no more than twenty or thirty braves riding protectively wide on the flanks of the train, and M'Grea guessed that even these would turn out to be fledgling warriors along with some old braves of the tribe.

And that was something to make him think. When a tribe moved to new hunting grounds, as tribes were always doing, it was usual for the braves to travel *en masse* with their families, because it was during a tribal move that they were weakest and most exposed to any enemy attack.

'Where'n the tarnation are the braves?' was the question that was beginning to hammer within Big M'Grea's mind. 'And — why the panic?'

Because clearly the column was in a panic. Truly they could be said to be fleeing. Squaws were dragging on the lead ropes to help the dogs with their burdened litters — those twin poles that were cleverly harnessed to the dogs, long poles that trailed on the ground, bent under the weight of thirty or forty pounds of blanket robes, tepee skins and Indian treasures, so that they slid like sledge runners through the dust and over the sage brush.

As they came nearer M'Grea could hear the shrill cries of the womenfolk as they urged the dogs and their few old horses into greater speed. The children were burdened, even the tiny three-year-olds, and their mothers weren't sparing them, either.

M'Grea lifted his eyes to the distant horizon, speculating. These Apaches weren't making a voluntary move to new hunting grounds. They were being driven out of the old ranges. And the question was — who was driving them out?

The Apaches were as fierce as most Indians, brave and savage fighters. They didn't allow themselves to be driven out of good camping grounds easily. So — who could it be, so far west, to challenge their right to the range they were occupying?

There was no answer to the problem just then. That distant horizon was devoid of humans, white or red, that he could see. But whatever was happening over that skyline affected Big M'Grea because he had to pass over it with his two prisoners.

When the Indians were no more than two hundred yards away, Big M'Grea shifted so that his eyes looked fully upon the silent, sullen men below him. There was a four-day scrub on

M'Grea's sun-blackened face, and it made him look tougher, fiercer than ever. It had been hard going, all the way from distant California, and the vast northern desert had been no picnic. Now their faces showed it, and slowed the elemental hardness that had kept them riding along when it might have been easier to have given up the battle against sun and windswept sand.

M'Grea said: 'There's Injuns comin' up the trail. Mostly squaws an' papooses, but with enough braves to give us a haircut ef we don't watch out. An' their horses is fresh.' He looked at their own drooping, sorry beasts. 'We gotta lie low an' hope they'll pass without seein' us. It ain't no good thinkin' we c'n run races with 'em — we can't.'

Dutch George snarled: 'The hell M'Grea, you give us our guns. You can't keep us hog-tied when we might have to fight fer our lives!'

M'Grea spoke flatly. 'You're gettin' no guns. Not just yet, anyhow. You think I was born yesterday?' he asked sardonically.

Dutch swore. 'Goddam, just now we'd use 'em agen the Injuns.'

'Sure. But you'd save one bullet for me, wouldn't you?' He shrugged contemptuously. He knew the moment he gave them their guns he signed his own death warrant. Win or lose against the Indians, Dutch or King would smack a bullet into him, maybe even just as soon as they got guns in their hands.

King Rattler hadn't spoken. He had sharper wits than Dutch, the German immigrant from Galveston. He'd known the futility of asking for guns from a man as wide-awake as Big M'Grea. He was biding his time cunningly for a more promising moment, and he knew it would come. One thing was certain, he wasn't going to be taken back to Stampede, that cow-town on the Rio Brazos. He wasn't going to decorate no gallows tree, not King Rattler!

Rattler wasn't his real name. He probably had some first name like Fred or Lem or Dave, but no one ever used it. For a long time he had been known simply by his surname, King, then someone in a fit of temper had given him the name of Rattler because he was dead poisonous.

King Rattler fitted well. M'Grea, keeping an eye on the pair as well as watching the advancing column, thought how like a vicious, deadly snake the fellow was. He was thin where Dutch was gross — a lean, evil figure with a habit of keeping his head stooped which further heightened the illusion of a watchful, brooding snake. He had mean brown eyes — so darkly brown they were nearly black — which held the same spiteful glitter that was in a cornered rattler's. Just now the blue-black growth on chin and top lip made him look particularly treacherous.

Watching him, M'Grea thought, 'That fellar's sure storin' up pisen fer me. Guess I'd better keep my eyes skinned whar he's concerned. He's up to any tricks, that mean *hombre*.'

Dutch George, for all his crude ferocity and greater bulk, wasn't to be feared as much as the slinky, evil King Rattler. M'Grea looked at the distant skyline and wondered what it contained for him. It was going to be tough enough, keeping an eye constantly on his two tricky companions without encountering any further perils beyond that heat-hazy horizon.

Then the Indians came up fast, still frantically trying to put as much distance as possible between them and their unknown enemies in the rear. The column came level with their hideout and less than a hundred yards from them, and then started to pass.

But the danger did not come from the shrill-voiced squaws and children with their dogs and pack horses. The mounted circle of braves was where the peril lay.

One wide-riding warrior passed well

behind without seeing them where they lay in this hot little gulch. But three more were moving in a line which would bring them very close if not within sight of them.

M'Grea's Sharps rifle came round to cover the danger. His shirt was clinging sweatily to his mighty shoulders; salt drops ran into his eyes and into the corners of his mouth, but he never moved, never stirred a muscle as he squinted towards the approaching near-naked warriors.

Below him, because their lives depended on it, the two killers held the heads of the three horses in an effort to keep them still and quiet. Perhaps, fortunately for them, their mounts were so travel-jaded they hadn't much interest in anything just then, not even in greeting their own kind; they stood and drooped as if the torrid, sun was like so much weight upon their sweat-rimed backs.

Two Indians branched off, again going deeper to the rear, for the moment, anyway, cutting off any chance of escape that way.

The third rode straight into the gulch.

He came trotting in, the picture of alertness as he sat easily, naturally upon his bare-backed pony. He rode with the single head-rope that served as bridle nipped between his knee and the horse's side, leaving his hands free to hold his long gun.

It was a flintlock, probably four feet in length — a Kentucky long gun, crude but very efficient. And the way he held it balanced between his brown hands, Big M'Grea guessed that the brave knew how to use it.

The Sharps rifle swung to cover the Indian. M'Grea didn't pull trigger, wouldn't pull trigger unless he had to. King Rattler's mouth was open in a tight round 'o', as if trying to hold himself in at sight of this danger that came trotting in on them.

Dutch George hadn't the same restraint. He saw death in that long gun, death for himself, and he suddenly shouted hoarsely: 'Give him der lead, M'Grea!' unable to keep quiet any longer. And in the excitement of the moment it was noticeable that his German accent came out strongly.

The battle-wise Indian promptly kicked bare heels into the ribs of his pony and sent it rearing in a flurry of hooves. His gun came up, searching.

M'Grea shot him. He did it reluctantly, because it betrayed their presence to the mob of Indians beyond. But there was nothing else for it.

He saw the long gun come glinting level, and it seemed to be pointing to where he lay exposed against the slope of ground. He sighted, and even the Indian's manoeuvre of bucking his pony didn't affect his aim. He squeezed trigger, and the lead spanged across and found its mark, so that though the long gun fired it was only in consequence of the nervous reflex of a dead finger on the trigger.

M'Grea came jumping stiff-legged down the slope, drawing his Bowie knife as he came. 'Start ridin',' he rapped, and ripped his knife through the bonds around the gunmen's legs. Then he plunged across and grabbed the Indian pony almost before its rider had come toppling from it. A fresh mount was just what he needed at that moment.

But M'Grea didn't go racing off to save his own skin. The thought didn't even occur to him. He swung across the plunging, bare-backed beast and pulled it whirling round so as to give the two gunmen chance to spur their weary mounts down the gulch. Then he reached out and grabbed the rein of his own tired horse and led it after the pair.

M'Grea had brought his men close on eleven hundred miles as his prisoners. He was less than a hundred miles from home now, and he wasn't going to lose them after all that weary labour.

The other horses gamely started a

gallop, but M'Grea knew that it wouldn't last long. His own restive, nervous little mount kept easily up with them, in spite of the unaccustomed weight it bore.

He swung round in the saddle. Already they were out of the gulch and in full view of the retreating column of Indians. He saw the mounted braves detach themselves from the main body and come streaking across towards them, flat on their ponies' backs. Even in that instant he saw that few had guns, and that was surprising, because usually the best-armed men were put to defending the squaws and papooses.

Then he turned his head, just as the two braves who had gone circling to the rear came riding swiftly over the shoulder of a hill to their left.

M'Grea fired — and missed. His mount hadn't the trained steadiness of a cow pony, and though they weren't going fast the horse ran too unevenly to permit of accurate marksmanship.

It was then that a surprising thing

happened. M'Grea was looking towards the two approaching Indians on their flank, because they were nearer and much more dangerous. He saw them suddenly wheel, and then one lifted a hand and signalled. At once the main bulk of horsemen riding in from the train pulled hard on their horses' heads, and in another second were riding slowly back to their former stations around the moving column.

M'Grea slackened pace and then shouted to his companions to slow down. There was no need to blow their mounts unnecessarily, and now there seemed no need to run away.

The two Indians on their flank had halted and were sitting their horses at a distance. But plainly they were no longer a threat; they were acting as guards to prevent any attack on the column by the three white men.

King Rattler understood the manoeuvre also, and dropped his mount into a walk, calling to Dutch George to do likewise. When M'Grea drew level,

Rattler said: 'That's shore queer. I don't figger it out none at all. That's the first time I've seen Injuns throw up three paleface scalps so easy.' He spat into the dust. 'An' they could have had our'n in fifteen minutes at the outside at the cost of no more'n a few braves.' He spat again, squinting back across the coarse brush to where the silent Indians sat their ponies. 'Me, I don't get it,' he said eventually.

M'Grea said grimly: 'Neither do I. Unless maybe they figgered three paleface scalps wasn't so important as fifteen minutes o' time. Unless maybe they reckon they need every brave they've got without losin' a few fer a bit o' white man's hair.'

He was looking towards the hills over which the fleeing Apaches had come, and he was wondering what it was that could inspire such great fear in their savage hearts.

'It sure must be powerful bad medicine fer Apaches,' he told himself, and then looked to see if there was any way of circling the danger area. But there was none. That way only the great mountain range had broken into low hills and easily negotiable passes. That was the only way through to the green Colarado river basin. Whatever lay beyond those hills had to be met.

They rode on, occasionally changing horses so as to rest them in turn, now that they had a spare mount. And obstinately, once again Dutch George growled a request for guns and M'Grea ignored it.

Dutch wasn't a deep thinker; there was no subtlety where he was concerned. He couldn't think beyond getting a gun into his hand for just one minute. To that end he was prepared to lie and give a word that would be broken at the first opportunity.

M'Grea knew his man and wasn't to be taken in. He knew Dutch was full of low cunning, and deceit, and he kept an eye on him.

But even more he kept watch on the drooping, glittery-eyed King Rattler.

For he knew that when the Rattler struck it would come without warning, swiftly, viciously — and killingly. He thought again how easy it would be to kill the two-legged reptile and be satisfied with that — satisfied and safe. But he hadn't ridden the trails into distant Southern California, through New Mexico, Arizona, and even touching Nevada, just to make a corpse of the killer.

King Rattler was worth two hundred and fifty dollars to him alive, and nothing dead. And two hundred and fifty dollars was a mighty lot of money to have — when you doubled it with the bounty on Dutch George's murdering head it made a tidy fortune in those days.

They lay up that night in an arroyo that had a faint crop of grass to it, a sure sign they were nearing water. M'Grea didn't know this country at all, for they were travelling south of the route he had taken when he had gone out trailing the killers those many weeks ago. But he decided to risk it — that grass held promise of tributaries of the Rio Colorado fairly near — and they finished the last of their precious water supplies before bedding down, hungry and fireless, for the night.

Next morning M'Grea dragged them reluctantly to their weary feet even before first light. They could make good ground while there was still a pleasant night chill in the air, and maybe in that time they would find water.

And if not? M'Grea reckoned they could keep going for a full day before giving in, and by that time he was certain they would come up with water.

He hadn't reckoned with the enemy that the Apaches feared so much that they were in flight from it now. They came upon them almost as soon as the yellow sun had lifted its flaming, angry head above the scorched yellow Eastern mountains.

They were riding close together, M'Grea and the spare mount on the heels of the drooping dejected killers.

The sun was blisteringly hot on their backs and heads, and it came reflecting up in fierce waves from the bare, sandy soil under their weary horses' hoofs. Their eyes ached from the strain of staring against the intense bright light, while their tongues lolled so dry they made scratching, scaly sounds when they moved them in their mouths.

Suddenly M'Grea pulled back on his horse. The heat from the desert distorted things, so that mighty rocks appeared to be cut in two at the base and shimmered and danced in the haze.

But M'Grea was used to it, could see beyond the tricks of desert heat waves.

And now he saw a face staring at them from behind rocks. A face with broad white bands painted on it, radiating from the nose to the ears and down through the mouth to the chin. A face with a single tonsure of coarse black hair tied up behind like a horse's tail.

A Comanche! And more than one!

The West's most savage, cruel,

reckless fighters. The Indians who alone of all tribes had refused to make peace treaties with the invading white man, who had resisted him so viciously that to date they had been left alone — Comanches who lived by hunting, and would share nothing with anyone outside their tribe, not even with their brother Indians such as the war-like Apaches.

M'Grea knew them. He had been prisoner of theirs for two days long ago. And it had been an awful experience.

So he killed this first Comanche almost without thinking. The gun smacked against his thigh, his finger triggered. And a painted brave went to the happy hunting grounds all in a fraction of a second.

Then M'Grea saw the second fierce, painted face — and a third. Saw that the way was barred to them down that valley. He was shouting to his prisoners to get off their mounts and find cover, when suddenly mounted

Comanches came streaking across the valley towards them.

This time it was M'Grea who had ridden into an ambush, and not the Indians.

2

The Town Called Dead End

Dead End sprawled on the north bank of the Rio Colorado, just where the vast Staked Plains reared as a mighty plateau, two thousand feet above sea level. It was a place of no importance, a huddle of blistered paint and warped woodwork that served a scattered community of a few hundred citizens.

But there were men who saw a future in Dead End, and claimed it to be not the dead end that the first settlers had christened it a few years before. Those were the men who had reconnoitred the Staked Plains beyond and had seen in the black soil the richest cattle land in the world — and the biggest. These men said that the famed Texan coastal plains, where cattle were reared by the hundred thousand, would count as nothing compared with those high, healthy grasslands, well-watered because they lay on the leeward side of the mighty Sierre Madre Occidental Mountains.

Already they were moving cattle up the broad Rio Colorado basin and staking out holdings on the plains, and news of the broad, fertile lands was spreading and attracting more men, and they were beginning to trickle through regularly now. Dead End was looking up.

But this day Dead End wasn't concerning itself with the future. History and posterity have little importance to a people fighting for their immediate existence, and there were citizens in Dead End who were saying that that was about it — they who had opened up the Dead End range were now having to battle for their lives.

Old Silver Sam was saying as much right now. He was close on seventy, and perhaps because his natural end was near, he had little fear of death. He stood up and spoke bluntly at this meeting called of the citizens of Dead End and surrounding country.

'We came here to settle an' build a place with a future fer our children,' he told them. He himself had changed from a miner in pursuit of elusive silver in far-distant Nevada to became a stock-raiser on the Colorado river. 'We made this place what is it.' He spat brown juice into the brass cuspidor that stood to the side of the bar in this saloon called Milligan's, though Milligan was a couple of years dead by now.

'It ain't much, I know,' he went on, 'but we done the hard work, I reckon, an' in a few years' time we'll all have nice holdings an' our folk'll inherit good pastures. That is, ef we have any holdin's left,' he ended sombrely.

He was a real old-timer — not so big, bent with long years of stooping underground, and as spare as a long life in a desert can make a man. He hadn't many teeth left, so that his face looked curiously squashed and tiny, but it was brown and looked healthy, and even the grey stubble on his chin didn't detract from his appearance. He looked the kind of man to be depended on, resourceful even in his old age, a match for nimbler men of less than half his years.

Now he looked round the saloon. Old Silver Sam had called the meeting, and around sixty people had come there that hot afternoon to listen to him. They were all men. A few women had wanted to come in and take part, but they had been politely escorted away.

For what Silver Sam wanted to talk to them about could easily degenerate into gunplay, and women were better out of the way when Samuel C. Colt added his voice to any argument.

All eyes were fixed on him. Mostly they were people from Dead End itself, men who owned businesses like Coogan, the corn chandler, Kurt Reimer, who kept the livery stable, Alf

York, who had the biggest store, and the Thomson brothers, who were just opening up in competition with him to get the new trade that was coming through Dead End.

But, in addition, there was a few nesters from just out of town, a few punchers from off the ranches who happened to be in town that day, and all the local landowners like Silver Sam Hayday himself. You expected ranchers to attend such a meeting, of course, because mostly what was to be discussed affected them. Not that they were big landowners, except for the Laramie brothers.

There were other men there at that meeting, too — men like the half-Mexican Durango and the flaxen-haired Swede Nils Perhof, gamblers both. And Jimmy Maxill, Nick Wade, and Rope Coltas, who liked to sit around all day and play cards, and would do anything, even to killing a man, to satisfy his demand for leisure. And others, some of them nearly as bad as the trio of professional gunmen.

Others including Jed Louen, known behind his back as Loco Lou, because if he wasn't crazy, then most other men weren't sane.

And it was on Loco Lou, with his perpetual smile that showed clean, white even teeth and made his light blue eyes look like chips of sparkling ice — it was on Loco Lou that Old Silver Sam's gaze rested longest.

His strong old voice rang out, though the saloon wasn't all that big that it needed him to shout to be heard just then. There was no one else talking, and that showed how important matters were for the saloon to be so quiet at that time of day.

'Yeah,' he said, 'I guess way things are there sure won't be many left to enjoys the fruits of their labours. Ef we're not careful, I guess we'll all be driven from our lands.'

Burt Laramie, oldest of the three Laramie brothers who had come to own so much in the past year, stirred.

His voice was amused, but there was an edge to it.

'Reckon you wouldn't be thinkin' that the Laramie brothers is doin' any drivin',' he said.

Old Silver Sam faced him squarely.

'I ain't sayin' anythin' about the Laramie brothers — about anyone, fer that matter. All I know is that one by one the old settlers is losin' their lands, an' the Laramie brothers is always successful in buyin' them up.'

And that was true. Dan Edgar had been first to go. He had had some good grassland on both sides of a strong-running tributary of the Rio Colorado that never dried up even in the most rainless of years. It was land to be coveted.

Dan stopped coveting it in his fortieth year. That was when they found him with his neck broken.

It could have been that he had been thrown from his mount, of course, but men whispered that bruises don't show on the neck when a fellar falls on his head. Not usually. But if a man was to have a gun slashed across it from behind, or a loaded stick — well, maybe then a bruise would show.

The Laramies got that land cheap.

And holding the Edgar tributary, the Laramies also held the water supply to two more rather small ranches. Dan had always let them water at his stream, but now the Laramies shot down any cattle that came near. Within a week, with cattle dying like flies, the two ranchers had to give in. And the Laramie brothers bought their lands *dirt* cheap this time; for who wants a ranch without water?

But matters didn't end there, as brave old Silver Sam told them right now.

'We're almost at war, round Dead End,' he said bluntly. 'Ranchers — aye, an' nesters, too — are losin' their herds to rustlers, their men are bein' shot at so that it's as much as a rancher can do to find men willin' enough to work for him. I guess some of us can't hold out much longer. I guess there'll be more land up fer sale shortly.'

Burt Laramie drawled: 'When that time comes, pardner, you jest let me know. I'm land hungry. I want all I c'n get, an' I'm prepared to make top bid for it.'

They were beginning to square off in that saloon now. Men knew the implication of things without words being spoken, and those who sided with Silver Sam came alongside him to give him their support.

And behind the three Laramie brothers, burly, well-fed, and arrogantly confident, ranged Durango and Perhof, the gamblers, Maxill, Wade, and Rope Coltas, and other men who lived by their guns. And still other men who were instinctively against what Silver Sam was proposing to do, because they knew it was not to their advantage.

And with the crowd behind the Laramie brothers was the easy-smiling, blue-eyed man who was known as Loco Lou.

There was a third party, of course. There always is at such meetings. They're the people who didn't want to show their hands — people who wanted things badly but weren't prepared, as old Silver Sam was prepared, to suffer maybe in attaining their desires.

And today in Milligan's Saloon the third party was vastly in the majority. For the Laramie brothers were known to be ruthless, were known to be capable of any brutal act when they were crossed, and these small, hard-working men had enough on their hands without bringing wrath from the big landowners, too.

Old Silver Sam caught on the last, ironic words of Burt Laramie.

'Sure you'll make top bid,' he said bluntly. 'An' why? Because no one else'll dare bid agen you!'

Burt Laramie half-started out of his chair, and then he eased back, laughing contemptuously. It was true, but he couldn't be bothered to silence the voice that spoke the truth. Not just then, anyway.

Men stirred uneasily at Silver Sam's blunt words, and then they relaxed as Burt Laramie relaxed. For they had feared too much action, with that powerful party standing behind the cattleman's chair.

But Silver Sam didn't give a hang about action. He was wanting action; in fact, that was why he had called this meeting. He went on just as bluntly to say:

'I figger it's time men were pertected, so that others will dare stand up an' make bids. I figger even beyond that — that there shouldn't be no need fer men to have to sell up because they've been driven off the land. So what I'm proposin' now is that we do what we should have done a good time ago in Dead End.'

'And that is?'

The gambling breed called Durango asked the question, but it was a matter of form. Everyone had heard by now what was in old Silver Sam's mind.

'We bring the law into Dead End.'

Cal Laramie, second of the Laramie brothers, now spoke. His voice, too, held the humour that had been in Burt's. They were powerful men, and confident in their wealth and strength.

'We wouldn't know what ter do with law ef it came an' settled here,' he said, and at that crude sally there was a guffaw from the Laramie faction. When it had subsided he demanded: 'You aimin' to appoint a sher'f?'

Silver Sam nodded.

'You're dead right, I am. It's time this town grew up. First sign of growin' up's to get yourself a sher'f, I reckon, so I say let's appoint one here an' now.'

There were murmurs of approval at that, and some came from the middle party though it was done covertly, so that the Laramies wouldn't know who was applauding.

'We got need fer law,' went on Silver Sam. 'God knows we need it in Dead End! There are wolves an' lambs in this hyar place, an' I reckon ef we ain't careful the wolves'll sure gobble up what's left o' the lambs in no time. We need law to pertect us — we want a sher'f who will ride out an' put an end to all this cattle-stealin' an' back-shootin' an' fence bustin'. I propose, then, we elect a sher'f an' give him all powers to bring law into Dead End.'

A score of voices lifted in a growling 'Aye!' at that. But Burt Laramie gave no heed to them; he came slowly out of his chair, big, well-dressed, well-fed, the picture of power.

'We want no sher'f in Dead End,' he said flatly, 'an' we ain't goin' to have such nonsense. Ef a fellar can't look after hisself, I reckon he ain't got no right to call hisself a Texan, that's all.'

His contemptuous remark brought a quick, growling response from his supporters, and from many in that big third party that still hung undecided along the walls between the two main factions. For there were many who lived in this cowtown only because they had fled from the law farther back east.

Durango, who was cunning and quick with his mind, as befitted one who followed a gambler's calling, suddenly spoke up.

'I guess I'm fer havin' a sher'f, too,' he said.

Three Laramies whirled on him, surprised but threatening. And with them, growling anger against the gambler they had thought to be one of their party, came the others. But not Jed Louen, the man with the white even teeth and loco smile. He was watching old Silver Sam as if fascinated.

Durango said smoothly: 'Sure, I think we oughta have a sher'f. An' me, I reckon I'm gonna propose a right good man fer that office right now. I give you the name of the man I think fittest fer the job.'

He paused. They waited for the name. It came.

'Jed Louen!'

For a second there was silence, and then Burt Laramie burst out laughing, to be followed by the rest.

'The hell, that's good!' Burt roared. 'That's a good one, Durango. Fer a minute you had me guessing.' And he laughed again, for to suggest that vicious Loco Louen should be made sheriff seemed downright good humour to his sardonic mind.

Silver Sam quietened the disapproving growl that rose from his followers. 'That's funny, Durango, I reckon,' he said sarcastically. 'But we ain't hyar fer fun, I guess. We mean business, we people who're tired of mob rule an' violence. I'm goin' to make a serious proposal.'

He looked round at his followers, and there was a twinkle in his eyes. 'I'm goin' to propose as sher'f an old useless sourdough who ain't got much time left on earth — me, Silver Sam Hayday!'

They stirred all around him, muttering uneasily at that. They knew that old Sam wasn't out office-hunting. He didn't want to wear a sheriff's badge because it was pretty. They knew that Sam was making this proposal because the job carried danger, and he had less dependents probably than any man there. In fact he only had one — a granddaughter — and he'd already made provision for her in case things happened to himself.

Coogan, the corn chandler and an old friend of Silver Sam's, said: 'You're too old, old-timer. Reckon this is a job fer a younger man.'

Silver Sam shook his grey head. 'Reckon we'll need all the younger men fer dep'ties. I guess I'm the only one with time enough ter make sher'fing a full-time occupation.'

He dismissed the reluctant protests of his friends and wheeled on the Laramie faction. 'As self-appointed chairman, I'm puttin' this to the vote. Those who want me as sher'f, put up their right hands.'

Some hands shot up immediately, then a few followed more slowly, as if their owners were a little doubtful of being seen publicly supporting the old-timer.

Sam counted. 'Fifteen,' he said. There was disappointment in his voice, and he looked disapprovingly at the uneasy third party who might have been expected to vote for him against Loco Lou.

'All right,' he said resignedly. 'Ef there ain't no more, all those in favour of Jed Louen signify with their right hands — an' you only got one right hand, in case you didn't know,' he added grimly.

The men back of the Laramie brothers lifted their hands. Sam saw that Louen was voting for himself. 'Sixteen,' he counted.

Burt Laramie came out of his seat quickly, jubilant. 'We got a sher'f,' he exclaimed. 'Jed Louen — old Loco hisself!' Jed Louen's head came smiling round at that. Only the Laramies dared call him Loco to his face. Burt Laramie momentarily checked himself, looking into those blue eyes, into that smiling, rather boyish face, but there seemed no malice there, no danger.

Then Silver Sam was shouting, 'No, he ain't. I guess I didn't vote fer myself like Lou did. So that makes us sixteen each — a tie!'

They were all on their feet in that saloon now. Alf York, middle-aged but courageous, a man flat-footed and fat from years behind a counter, called, 'Now what do we do, Sam?'

Burt Laramie was about to say something, and then he caught the look in Loco Lou's bright blue eyes and checked what he was about to say. For there was something in those eyes he had seen there before, and he was satisfied.

Jed Louen did it so slowly, so openly. His hand went down to his belt and came up with his gun. Very casually he flicked it, so that it broke open and he could check on the rounds in the breach; then he flicked with the wrist and it clicked shut.

The gun was pointing at old Silver

Sam. The finger calmly took pressure on the trigger. There was an explosion. Silver Sam went down in a sudden huddle, and everyone there knew that he would never rise again.

Jed Louen, he who was known as Loco Lou, laughed lightly. 'I bin wantin' to do that to the old buzzard ever since he opened his yappin' voice,' he said casually.

The callousness of his remark broke the spell that had gripped the men at the tragedy. There was a sudden growl of oaths, and hands started down for gun belts and holsters. And then they stopped, because Loco Lou had the drop on them and was smilingly inviting them to clear leather and start shooting. But they knew they hadn't a chance against that drawn gun.

Jimmy Maxill, Rope Coltas and Mick Wade had guns out supporting Louen, and other gunnies weren't far behind with theirs, either. It stopped any thoughts of a sudden sneak shot to cripple Louen.

Alf York rose from the side of old Silver Sam. 'He went out,' he said slowly. 'Old Sam got his'n then. He didn't have a chance.' He thought for a moment, as if wondering what to say, how far he dare speak his mind in face of those guns. Then he said, 'Mebbe some of us won't fergit how it happened, either,' and that was as much as he dared say just then.

Jed Louen's smile didn't alter a fraction. He seemed tolerantly amused by everything. 'I guess that deprives the opposition of their candidate,' he drawled. 'It also puts 'em one short ef they vote fer anyone else. So that seems to make me sher'f o' Dead End, don't it?'

The three Laramies came across. It tickled their sense of humour. Young Joe Laramie called, 'It sure does, Jed. This calls fer drinks on the Laramies, I reckon.'

'Sure,' said Burt in delight. 'An' the Laramies are gonna show their sense of responsibility as citizens. The Laramies are gonna provide the new sher'f with an office an' jail. Sure, an' a nice monthly pay packet until we fix up some sorta tax system like they always do when law an' order comes to a town. Open up them bottles — this is a day to celebrate!'

They were celebrating riotously — even many of the third party who had been doubtful about voting in public — when Alf York, Coogan and Reimer came out carrying the still figure of brave old Sam Hayday.

And far out in the scrub foothills, Big M'Grea was fighting for his life — fighting to get out of the Indian ambush and make his way with his prisoners to the nearest water supply.

The nearest water supply — It was a town called Dead End on the north bank of the Rio Colorado. A cowtown with a crazy sheriff.

3

The Comanche Invasion

Big M'Grea had a voice to match. Now it bellowed, 'Off'n them hosses! Git cover!'

They fell off. M'Grea saw them scrabbling for cover, had a momentary impression of Dutch George's fat, blue-chinned face snarling back an appeal for a gun he wasn't going to get.

Then M'Grea fired.

He'd seen a chance and taken it, all in a fraction of a second.

There were seven mounted braves in this party, with more in the background across the valley from them. They came screaming in from a range of no more than fifty yards, hair streaming, tomahawks and guns raised in deadly intent, their brown, naked bodies glistening in the yellow light of the new-risen sun.

Suddenly the leading pony began to run slightly across. It was a habit common to all Indian ponies, because they never wore blinkers or eye shades of any kind, and they liked to see where they were going and that meant turning the head so as to look squarely forward out of one eye. And turning the head can throw a pony slightly out of a straight run.

M'Grea saw the opportunity — and grasped it. His finger tightened on the Sharps; a bullet spanged across and that pony went silently down into the dust, throwing its rider into a rolling, scrambling ball among the scrub.

Three other ponies crashed in a frantic mêlée of tossing manes and kicking hoofs, unable to get out of the way of their stricken companion, and the remaining three riders had to pull hard and away in order to escape being pulled down also.

It spoilt the surprise element of that ambush; it gave M'Grea a few valuable seconds and he took full advantage of them.

He came to a kneeling position, Sharps laid alongside his cheek. Gunpowder fumes whipped back into his face as he triggered off a fleeting bullet that smacked the life out of one of the three braves. The others started to charge again, but M'Grea shifted his aim and a second toppled screaming from the bare back of his mount.

The third somehow escaped the next bullet and was through and upon them. M'Grea came rising up to his full height. He saw that savage painted face grinning triumphantly down at him, saw the lean brown arm with the raised tomahawk. Then he threw himself backwards, just in time out of reach of that circling weapon as it crashed towards his face.

His rifle barked a moment before he smashed back on to his broad shoulders. The Indian went riding on, but there was a strange expression on his white daubed face. It was the expression which says, plainer than words, 'This can't be true. It can't have happened to me!' But it had. Ten paces further and that pony was carrying a corpse for a rider, a corpse which somehow stuck on until the terrified pony reared at a snake in its path and tossed it from its back.

But it did some damage, that frightened pony. It ran among M'Grea's party's horses and communicated its fear to them. M'Grea couldn't turn to look, but he heard shrill whinnying, heard the clatter of unshod hoofs on the sun-scorched bare rocks, and then their beasts went racing crazily back into the arid mountains.

He killed another Indian, just crawling to his feet. Right now he hadn't time to think about their horses.

About a dozen braves were streaming across to join in the fight, and the foremost were almost up to their stricken companions by now. The three who had been unhorsed had rolled under cover. Two had guns, and these now opened fire.

King Rattler had started to work his way up the rocky hillside, where loose stones made a precarious footing for even the sure-footed ponies, and the heavy, sweating, cursing Dutch came up close after him.

M'Grea saw and approved the manoeuvre and came crabbing quickly behind. He emptied his gun into the approaching mass, then started to reload on the run, ducking and dodging behind the piled stone masses in order to keep away from the badly aimed Indian bullets. They were jumping from their ponies and starting to come swiftly up the stony hillside after them, when M'Grea dropped behind a boulder and pointed the hot barrel of his gun at the warriors.

Two got hit and went writhing down into the desert dust, and the other braves saw sense and hurled themselves into cover.

M'Grea retreated up the hillside,

firing occasionally to keep the Comanches from starting up a charge again. And then he heard the Rattler's voice: 'Doggone it, we come a bad way!'

He screwed his head. The Rattler and Dutch were sprawled behind a rocky outcrop higher up the hillside. For the moment he couldn't see what was stopping their retreat. He triggered twice more, started to reload and called, 'What's holdin' you?'

Dutch's snarling voice — 'A damn' great gulch! We can't go no further this way, M'Grea. Blast it, we're trapped!'

M'Grea picked a good position and wormed his way across to the cover. All right, they were trapped! Well, he had a Sharps which said that some of his old enemies, the Comanches, would go out before he did.

He reloaded just as the Indians rushed for nearer cover. A bullet zipped off the rock in front of his eyes, and stone splinters whipped up and peppered his face. He fired. The Indians went down.

They didn't charge after that. They were war-wise, those braves, and they came crawling nearer, cleverly taking advantage of the cover which until now had been in the white man's favour.

M'Grea smacked back viciously every time he caught a hint of movement, but he never hit after that though the bullets kept the braves moving cautiously and slowly.

He looked across the narrow defile, his eyes mere slits as he stared into the fiery morning sun that burned the life out of these scarred and rugged foothills. The sweat ran down his powder-blackened face, tasting bitter when it oozed between his parched lips. He was thinking, 'All this way — and now it ends here, in this hell-hole!'

Dutch hadn't given up trying. His voice floated across to M'Grea. 'M'Grea, you gotta give us our guns! Mebbe we'd stand a chance of there was three guns agen them varmints.'

M'Grea didn't answer him. He was thinking, 'Mebbe they might stand a chance ef I did, him an' the Rattler. But I don't reckon I would.'

He had no illusions. Give them guns and mebbe even the first bullet would come back to settle his life. Better take on the Injun pack himself, he thought grimly.

An Indian screamed and flung himself at them from near cover. M'Grea hardly looked at him as he smacked lead into his fanatic face. He was staring down the valley, and his eyes were wide now with dismay.

For flooding into the valley was an army of mounted braves, horses' manes flying in the morning sun, weapons glinting as they came streaming towards the fight.

M'Grea heard Dutch's thick voice exclaim hoarsely, 'Goldarn it, look there! This is where we get our'n!'

But M'Grea was pumping away at the Comanches. They had risen abruptly from cover at sound of the advancing horsemen. The big puncher had a feeling that he should be remembering something; he felt that this wasn't quite right, the way those Comanches were rising to their feet.

For now they were staring back down the valley. They weren't charging forward in jubilation.

And then M'Grea understood. No plumes — no feathered headdresses.

These couldn't be Comanches! These could only be — Apaches! — who never used such ornaments.

Apaches! The braves who had left their squaws and papooses to make that terrified trek alone! M'Grea understood it all now. The dreaded Comanches had come circling down from the north, driving the Apaches from their hunting grounds. Those fleeing Apaches were trying to escape butchery at the hands of their savage Indian brothers — their menfolk had stayed behind to fight a rearguard action so as to give them time to escape.

And now here they were, pouring back in headlong flight before the victorious Comanches.

And M'Grea suddenly understood the significance of the ambush they had run into. This band of Comanches must have circled the Apaches' rear, intending to trap them when they tried to break back to their people, and they, M'Grea and his prisoners, had blundered in on the ambush.

The only thing was, in blundering they had unwittingly saved the defeated Apaches; for now the trap was sprung and the way was clear for them to thunder through the valley.

M'Grea heard Apache screams. They had sighted the small group of Comanches on the hillside. He shouted to his prisoners, 'We've got a chance. These are Apaches. Keep down out of sight. Mebbe they'll ride through without knowin' we're here at all!'

His heart was pounding. It looked as though these Apaches in turn were going to save them from the Comanches.

They did. When he peered cautiously out he saw the Comanches rushing for their ponies, while the beaten Apaches came racing up at this opportunity for vengeance, however limited, upon their hated Comanche enemies.

The Comanches were overrun. They fought savagely, bravely, fought while there was life in them. But in a matter of seconds two hundred Apaches had flooded over them and hacked them to pieces.

It hardly caused the retreating Indians to pause, they were in such overwhelming strength. For one second the shock as they ran into the barely-mounted Comanches caused a ripple of hesitation to run down the long line of Apaches; the next they were all over their enemies and streaming in full flight up the valley towards the mountain ranges over which M'Grea had just brought his prisoners.

For about a minute after the Apaches had left the valley, there was a silence that was broken only by the sound of fast-retreating hoofs.

And then the Comanches came. They

came wheeling swiftly up the valley, lusting to destroy the demoralized Apaches. And watching them tear by, naked brown bodies clinging closely to their bare ponies' backs, M'Grea gasped with astonishment.

Three or four hundred Comanches were flooding into the valley!

It took them minutes to get through, and when they were gone there was a high yellow cloud of dust floating over the trail.

M'Grea heard Dutch's thick voice, 'See them Injuns? Hundreds of 'em; I've never seen so many in all my days!'

But M'Grea was looking back down the valley and saying to himself, 'If there's three or four hundred in this war-party, how many Comanches are there back with the tribe?'

Because Comanches never left their squaws and papooses unprotected. This would be a war-party only, with the main strength of the tribe coming up with the weaker element. The thought in M'Grea's mind was, 'How many in all?' And — 'What are they doin' here, so far south, in such strength?'

It could mean only one thing, he decided. War! War upon the white man who was moving ever deeper into the great American continent. Perhaps they had been roused to fight once more against the paleface because of the recent pioneering on the great Staked Plains, the richest hunting grounds for Indians in the West. The Indian was defending almost the last territory left to him in all America.

They waited half an hour, during which time M'Grea's eyes picked out a possible trail across the hillside. He didn't intend to set off afoot down that valley, with the likelihood of the Comanches returning and catching up with them.

When it seemed safe he gave the word, and started the prisoners off before him. They cursed because they hated walking, as all Texans hate it, but they went willingly all the same because they knew the alternative.

With grim humour M'Grea thought that, in fact, there were several alternatives, but they all led up to the same end — death. Death at the hands of the Comanches if they stayed and were discovered; death from thirst if they didn't find water — and frightful death if they blundered accidentally on to the main Indian mass, who would give them to the squaws for torture if they were captured alive.

They climbed, weary, thirsty, and aching. Two hours later they clambered over the hill and looked down upon the distant Rio Colorado basin, green and fertile, spread over with the cattle of the pioneering settlers.

And camped in a narrow defile at their feet they saw the main body of Comanches.

A town had sprung up, a town of tepees. Between the rows was constant activity as hundreds of people thronged to and fro about the domestic business of foraging for wood, keeping the fires going, cooking, eating — and making palaver, as Indian braves always do when out on the warpath.

Cautiously peering down, M'Grea thought: 'With the war-party we've just seen, there must be close on a thousand braves in the tribe.'

A thousand braves! Rarely in the history of the ill-organized Indians were so many braves gathered together at one time to face a common enemy, but here they were and their purpose was clear. They were intent on stopping the white man as he strode westwards across the American continent.

M'Grea said aloud: 'We gotta get through an' tell our people what's happenin' out here. Otherwise there's goin' to be something like a massacre all down this valley.'

Dutch growled: 'The hell with 'em! Let's go get some water.' His face was an unpleasant red above the blue scrub around his face. He looked what he was, a low, brutal animal. King Rattler was silent, but M'Grea thought he looked even more venomous.

He said wearily: 'OK, let's try'n make that water. But watch out for Injun scouts. I reckon that plain'll be stiff with 'em!'

They began the cautious crawl down the steep-sloping hillside. M'Grea was thinking: 'We'll be lucky if we make water in time.'

They were in a race against death — death from thirst. And the Indian scouts would be obstacles to slow them down and make the going more prolonged just at a time when speed was imperative.

They crawled on, onwards towards that rising, burning, killing-hot sun. On towards Dead End with its new sheriff — Loco Louen!

4

A Girl Called Bonnie

When Bonnie Haydays's tears were dry she took off her dress and put on her workaday jeans, then got on her horse and rode off for three days. She rode alone, but round her slim waist was a cartridge belt and in it a worn old Colt that was friend, protector, and chaperon all in one. It had been her grandfather's, the late Silver Sam Hayday's, one-time prospector and later cattle-owner.

At the end of the third day she quit. An awful feeling came to her that she was licked, but before she quite gave in she turned her horse across the mesquite and loped into Dead End. It was dark when she reached it, brawling and noisy under the Texan stars.

There was a light at the back of Alf York's store, warm and yellow and inviting to a rider tired from hours in the saddle. Bonnie got down stiffly, hitched her horse in the alley; then went and knocked at York's back door.

Alf opened up suspiciously, a lamp lifted in his left hand so that the rays fell out into the street. When he saw Bonnie, weary and caked with desert dust, he exclaimed: 'The land's sake, this is no place for you, gal!' and drew her quickly inside.

His wife came and clucked like a fussy hen.

'We thought you was goin' back East,' she kept saying. 'That's whar your gran'pappy sure intended you to go!' she said severely.

Bonnie stood in the living-room, tall and slim, her figure somehow taut as she surveyed the old couple, her young face etched with deep lines of bitterness and frustration.

'I'm not going back East,' she told them. 'Not yet. And I'm not selling out, either, so you don't need to start on that subject.'

But they were good friends, and they made allowance for her brittle tones because they knew how much she had loved that fine old silver prospector, Grandfather Sam Hayday. They knew the extent of the grief that held her now, and they respected her for it.

But Alf's eyes dropped to the gun she wore on her thigh, and his face grew troubled.

'What're you aimin' to do, Bonnie?' he asked slowly, his eyes still on that gun.

'I'm aimin' to bring some justice to Dead End, just like my — my grandfather aimed to do.' Slowly she took off her gloves, and her blue eyes looked less blue than usual, greyer, as if from weariness. 'I've stomped the country,' she went on bitterly. 'Tried everyone — ranchers, punchers, nesters — anyone who looked as though he might be sick of Colt law. I've talked to them, argued till I'm blue in the face

— and got nowhere with it!'

'Argued about what, honey?' asked Mrs York.

'I went around askin' people to get together an' run these no-good crooks and low-down murderin' *hombres* out of Dead End and set up law just like my grandfather wanted.'

'And not a man moved to help you?' Old Alf was walking heavily forward, his hand coming out.

Bonnie hesitated. 'Well, not quite. There were some who would have come, but they wanted others to come with 'em. But most were so scared they wouldn't do nothin' except say they'd do some thinking about it.' The girl's disgust exploded as she repeated it: 'Thinking! They won't even do that, once I'm out of the way!'

And then she stepped back quickly as Alf York's hand nearly closed over her gun.

'I want that gun, Mr York!' she snapped.

'That's how I reckoned it.' He nodded

heavily. 'You wouldn't be thinking of gunnin' fer Jed Louen, now would you?'

Bonnie relaxed. So old Alf York thought she was in town just to call out the new sheriff.

'I'm not planning on suicide,' she told him. 'Give me a chance, mind you, and Sheriff Louen will get what he deserves. But callin' him out — no!' She shook her head. A chicken might just as easily call out a grey wolf or a prairie fox. And Louen wouldn't hold his guns just because she was a girl.

Alf nodded approval.

'We like you too much to see you go an' get yourself liquidated,' he told her, then he went out to fetch in some of Silver Sam's old buddies to discuss the situation.

They sat around the pot-bellied stove that was cold this night, as it had been for over three months, but it felt natural and companionable to sit that way. And they talked into the small hours, seeking some solution to their problems.

Kurt Reimer, who loved horses even though one had lamed him long ago, and now kept Dead End's only livery stable — he summed things up in his heavy German accent.

'Der Laramies is too powerful. Mitt der gunmen an' gamblers an' bad mens in der town, der is too many who don't want law an' order. Some day it will come, but too many mens will die before that day. All der men you haff seen' — his pink, freckled hand waved as if to embrace the country over which Bonnie had ridden — 'dey don't wan' to be der first mens.'

And then he supplied the solution — he voiced the answer to their problem: 'We must a leader find to make men brave enough to face der Laramies.'

It was as simple as all that. Find a man that other men would follow.

Alf York knocked out his corn cob.

'Easier said than done!' he grunted. 'But where are we gonna find him?' He looked round at his stolid, pipe-smoking companions, tradesmen all. 'We're old Sam's best friends, the men who should be avengin' his murder. But we're not fightin' men. We're too old, too slow, an' besides we got wives an' children to think of, and that don't make you feel like leadin'.'

Coogan, the corn chandler, said cynically: 'Guess we've all got an excuse when it comes down to that, right to the last danged nester!' He shoved back in his chair, suddenly irritable. 'What's the good of talkin'?' he demanded. 'That's too many of 'em! An' they're killers, the whole blamed lot of 'em! That's why nobody's anxious to talk out o' turn whar the Laramies is concerned.'

Back came Kurt Reimer's flat, gutteral accents. 'It is what I said — we must get a man to lead us. You will see, find der man an' people will follow.'

And then, disconsolate, depressed, they went to bed, Bonnie bunking up at the Yorks' place.

She went out into Dead End the next day, but Alf York wouldn't let her wear her gun in public.

'Just in case you meet up with Loco Lou an' feel tempted to use it,' he told her, and this day meekly she surrendered it.

She was coming back from the forge, where she arranged for some work to be done when the blacksmith could get round to the Hayday spread — was just by the new sheriff's even newer office, when she saw the three men trudging in along the western trail.

Most of the loungers saw them at the same time, and because it was unusual to see men come in afoot from the vast western hinterland, they got curious and came crowding on to the verandas to look them over.

And Jed Louen came out of his office, too.

Bonnie turned and saw him, and the hatred that was foreign to her normally, tolerant, good-natured soul flared into an all-consuming rage within her. She had to step back into the protection of the Wells Fargo office in order to quell the violent trembling of her body at sight of her grandfather's murderer.

Perhaps it was as well. If Jed Louen had seen her, his twisted sense of humour might have thought to make sport of her before all those rough Dead End townsmen.

So she stood back in the shade, unobserved but observing. She saw Louen lounge easily down into the street and lean against the rail outside Milligan's. He was very sure of himself, but she noticed how his hands were always within inches of his belt. They called him Loco, but he didn't take chances.

He part-turned, and she saw that he was already wearing a crude silver star on his left breast. Turned, and she caught the flash of very even, very white teeth as his young face broke into that sudden smile of his. She thought, 'He's really good looking.' And he was, only you didn't think about that once you'd seen into those light blue eyes of his . . . seen the crazy, crackling mirth that was in them.

Eyes like that made you forget everything except questions of safety.

The newcomers were toiling into the one street that was Dead End now. Bonnie looked at them, shifting her burning, hating gaze from the quick-smiling new sheriff.

Two men walked together in front, with the third and biggest behind. One of the leading pair was lean and tall, but he walked with his head down, so that his face was in the shadow of his own dusty, battered black hat. His companion was a gross, shambling creature, tied up across the middle like a shapeless bundle of rags. He walked heavily, and his big, flat face was black with anger, while his lips moved as if in soundless cursing.

The third man — he who walked behind — was just as dusty, probably just as tired, but he didn't show it so much. He walked easily, a Sharps rifle tucked under the crook of his arm; and there was an air of watchfulness, a vigilance and caution about him that wasn't lost on the tough, knowing citizens of Dead End.

The Wells Fargo clerk was by Bonnie's side, green eyeshade shoved right back across his bald head so that it looked like a halo — a sight to startle in a place with a reputation like Dead End.

Bonnie heard the clerk's dry voice crackle:

'Them galoots ain't comin' this way because they want to. Looks like that big *hombre*'s a-kinda makin' 'em come to Dead End.'

And then she heard a postscript to that speech:

'Look at that fellar! That's a lot of man to get under one hat!'

Her attention drawn to him, Bonnie looked again at the man with the Sharps. She realized for the first time just how tall he was; then saw the breadth of those shoulders and felt, even though she couldn't see because of his shirt sleeves, the might of those muscles on his arms.

As the Wells Fargo clerk had said, there sure was a lot of man walking into town under that hat. A pretty tough, hardbitten *hombre*, too, by the way his eyes shifted to take in the spectators.

The big man with the Sharps must have said something, because almost outside Milligan's the two weary leaders of the party halted. Then it was that Bonnie noticed the absence of guns in the belts of the two first men. Her eyes flickered to the slim waist of the big man. He had guns all right, twin Colts in addition to his rifle.

It was a somehow tense, curious scene. The dusty trail, the warped and sagging buildings enclosing it, the burning morning sun blazing on to them — three silent, suspicious men, with a circle of shuffling loungers gradually closing in on them.

Then someone broke the silence. A scrub-faced, blood-shot-eyed denizen of Milligan's stated the obvious. 'You ain't got hosses.'

The leading pair stood, heads drooping, and said nothing. The big puncher with the Sharps said, drily:

'So that's why we took so long in comin' hyar. Thanks for pointin' it out, buddy!'

There was a little laugh at that, then Rube Thomson, who had opened a store in competition with Alf York's, said, 'How come you had to walk, stranger?' His voice was abrupt. He was brisk and businesslike and to the point in everything.

The big puncher took a water bottle off a prospector's mule that was hitched to Milligan's rail, drank, then handed it to his companions.

'Injuns,' he said laconically.

It startled his audience. There was a sudden ripple of oaths and exclamations at the word, and the Dead End loungers lost their ease and became taut with interest. Indians — the enemy since the white man set foot in America

— were on the prowl again.

'Many?' someone rapped. They didn't waste words, the people of Dead End.

'More Injuns,' the big man said slowly when his thirst was gone, 'than I've seen since we first came over the Alleghenys.'

That brought them right out, crowding forward. And then somehow that Sharps was pointing and though it didn't seem a definite menace they fell back before the long black barrel.

'Don't come too close,' Bonnie heard the big man say. 'I wouldn't like to lose my friends.'

And then, at that, they began to understand.

The man with the Sharps told them:

'You'd better watch out. Back in them hills is a thousand or more braves, and you don't get so many together all at one time unless they're on the warpath. My bet is they're goin' to try to keep back the white man so that he don't take the Staked Plains from 'em.'

'Apaches!' someone spat in contempt.

'Apaches?' The big man's eyes were slits against the brightness of the morning sun. 'No, sir, not Apaches. Comanches!'

Then they knew things were serious, all but the professional gunnies. Men who sell their guns as they did didn't waste shot on Indians, and so they didn't know much about Indians and Indian warfare. They were the men who followed behind the first waves of brave pioneers — the scum that rises to the top, all too often over the graves of the brave who have fought and made.

Jimmy Maxill, who had done most of his fighting within reach of a bar, laughed derisively.

'Now we got a new sher'f we don't need to get skeered of a few Injuns — not even Comanches!'

But the real settlers there, men like Alf York, Stamper, Josh Bealan and others, they knew there was no humour in the situation. Over a thousand

Comanches on the warpath was something. Something big and bad.

There was a sudden scatter of hooves and a man rode quickly away. Then two or three other horsemen went for their mounts and rode out of town in a wild flurry of dust and small stones.

Bonnie thought, 'That's Josh Bealan goin' to warn his boss at the One-by-One.' The others would be ranchers or punchers out to carry the warning of the Indian uprising to the outlying ranches where they lived and worked.

She thought, 'Maybe I'd better get back,' because the Hayday spread was pretty isolated, and a big bunch of Indians could burn it out in no time if they went on the rampage. Then she decided to stop a few minutes longer and see what happened about the trio.

Because she felt something was going to happen — everyone there sensed there was going to be drama, and few wanted to leave just yet.

For Sheriff Jed Louen had come lounging forward, so that he stood, grinning and insolently confident, before the three men. And where Sheriff Jed Louen was, so all too often was — tragedy.

Then Bonnie saw the head rising of the tall, lean man who stooped. The torn hat brim came up. She saw a small face, a face almost blackened by exposure — saw sharp, glittering, baleful eyes, eyes that were mean and vicious and vindictive. But just now, too, they held a look of cunning calculation; they ran swiftly over the faces of the crowding loungers — the roughnecks, the punchers and the just-ordinary folk who made up Dead End's population. Then they flickered with interest to a stop on Sheriff Louen's smiling, mocking face.

Bonnie's generous, loving spirit shrank in instinctive reaction against the antithesis of her own soul. This man, she knew immediately, was bad — bad as they come.

Her eyes now went back to the big puncher with them, looking at him with new interest. But his grey-powdered face didn't reveal anything of his character; he just looked hard, it was the face of a fighting man. And fighting men were sometimes bad as well as good, out there in Western Texas.

Jed Louen called: 'Hyar, pard.'

The big puncher looked at him before speaking, looked at the face and then at the badge as if they didn't match somehow. Bonnie had a sudden instinct that the big fellow wasn't to be taken in by badges, as some people were.

Then his voice came growling out of that big chest in a non-committal 'Hyar, sher'f.'

Bonnie saw that both the lean man and the scowling, swollen-bellied fellow with him were looking with interest at the sheriff. She wondered if they saw something there — recognized their kind. Birds of a feather, was the unspoken thought on her lips.

Louen's crazy eyes were dancing. Perhaps already he saw something to titillate his warped sense of humour.

'You aimin' ter stop over in Dead End?'

The big puncher looked the place over cynically. 'That the name you call it? Looks mighty appropriate ter me.'

Then he shook his head. 'We aim to lit out fer Stampede on the Rio Brazos — pronto. Just as soon as I c'n git hosses — '

Kurt Reimer's voice at once called across the heads of the crowd: 'You got money, stranger? Real money, *hein*? Not paper nor Continentals?'

The puncher nodded, but he wasn't taking his eyes off the smiling, lounging Sheriff Louen — a sheriff who carried slick, ornamented guns mostly seen on a quick-trigger fellar from the Border saloons.

'I got money. Dollars. Silver Mexes. An' British gold sovereigns. Enough fer three hosses, I reckon.' And then, for some reason, perhaps because he instinctively knew the type of men pressing closest around him, he called:

'Saddle 'em. I'll take what you give me, so long as they can make a hundred miles.'

Suddenly the Sharps shifted from his right to his left hand. That left his right hand free, and most men are a fraction faster in drawing right-handed than with their left.

Jed Louen saw — understood. And laughed. His grey eyes danced with unholy glee. But his words seemed innocuous enough as they slid between those white, even teeth of his:

'You kinda stickin' close to these *hombres*. Me, I'd say you was — bringing 'em in, huh?'

The puncher said nothing, but his eyes were alert for all they seemed nearly closed.

Louen lifted a match end to pick between his teeth. He was looking now at the tall, lean *hombre* with the battered black hat, and that *hombre* was looking straight at him.

'You a sher'f, too?' Louen's question came out suddenly.

The big puncher said 'Nope,' decisively — as if he didn't want to be a sheriff. And then someone spoke — the man with the small, sun-blackened face and glittering, malevolent eyes.

'He's a — bounty man!'

Somehow he spat out the last words, as if they were something that defiled his tongue — there was venom in the way he uttered them.

'A bounty man!'

The words rippled round the crowd. Bonnie, back up on the Wells Fargo loading platform, sensed the disgust and hostility of the crowd to the information, and in her own mind she shared it with them. Shared it, but at the same time had a sudden feeling of disappointment. She hadn't wanted this big, grim puncher with the fighting face to be a bounty hunter.

They were mostly lower than the vermin they hunted, the bounty men of the old West. When men spoke of bounty hunters they usually jeered: 'Set a thief to catch a thief!' But they really meant 'Set a killer.'

They were hard men, callous, brutal and ruthless, these bounty hunters. They went tracking down outlaws who had prices on their heads, living by the rewards they obtained. When a man sinned and was driven to flight out of the law-abiding areas, so these bounty men took to their horses in pursuit, following them into the wilder country where law hadn't yet caught up with the march of the Western pioneers. They weren't officers of the law; they had no authority vested in them at all. They were eager hungry mercenaries, who lived by tracking miscreants and bringing them in for the price on their luckless heads. The fact that the outlaws weren't commendable citizens didn't make people like bounty men any the better.

Bounty men and reptiles were coupled close together in normal men's minds.

Bonnie looked intently at the big puncher. He was the first bounty man she had met, though she had heard of many.

At the words the big puncher's hand had come inches closer to his Colt. A Sharps was a fine weapon out in the open, but for close work a Colt was king every time. And it seemed as though the bounty man anticipated close work any moment now.

'A bounty man?' Jed Louen looked at the two prisoners, a smile of amusement on his twitching lips. 'You aim ter take 'em in fer the reward on their hides?'

'That I do,' said the puncher flatly, and his voice was a low, hard challenge. He knew trouble was coming — but then he'd met with trouble almost every mile of that long journey back from the diggings in California.

Louen grinned round at his buddies. 'Guess I'll fix 'em in a nice new cell while you get yourself a sluice,' he said agreeably.

'I don't need no wash.' The bounty man's voice was ironic. 'I'll stay as I am.' He'd heard of sheriffs taking over prisoners before — and getting the reward. It was thought to be good humour, out West. You let a bounty man do the work, then step in and get the prize from him right at the last. It seemed right enough to everyone except the bounty man, because public opinion was dead against his calling.

Kurt Reimer came limping out with three saddled horses. The bounty man's eyes flickered over them: Kurt called 'They're good hosses, stranger. They'll get you there.'

The bounty man started to walk back a few paces towards them.

'They'd look better if they'd got strength to breathe once in a while,' he said mildly, and that brought a guffaw against Reimer.

The bounty man paid no heed to the laughter. Instead he jerked his head towards the horses. 'Git mounted,' he ordered, and the snarling, bad-tempered *hombre* made a step towards the drooping, dejected beasts. But the other, the mean-faced galoot, didn't move. He was looking at the sheriff, looking and waiting.

The sheriff nodded slightly, almost as if to convey a message to him. Then his lazy, insolent voice drawled: 'Hold up, there — bounty man!'

The big puncher halted in mid-stride, his eyes on the sheriff, cold and calculating. 'Yeah?' he asked softly.

'I reckon ter keep these men hyar a while until I know what they're supposed to have done. Guess I'm sher'f hereabouts, an' I don't reckon ter let galoots come marchin' prisoners across my territory.'

He was grinning. So were the gunmen and gamblers who formed his supporters. This was the sort of crazy humour they expected from their new sheriff. Pinching prisoners from a bounty man was right good fun at any time, but when the *hombre* that did the pinching was Loco Lou, then the humour was nearly hysterical.

The big puncher said nothing, just

turned and faced the sheriff squarely, legs braced apart and slightly bent. The crowd back of him and Lou began to move quickly out of line of possible fire.

Jed Louen eased close up to the big *hombre*, face agrin. He was confident, sure that he could take 'em all on, no matter how big they came.

He said:

'You hear, pard? I'm a takin' 'em off'n you.'

The reply was so soft that many in that crowd didn't hear it. But Bonnie did, just caught it as the words drifted through the bright hard sunshine towards her.

'You're not big enough — *hombre!*'

Those that heard gasped; for the bounty man had been deliberate in that insult. It was fighting talk, a demand for gunplay. And no demand for Colt talk ever went unheeded with Loco Lou.

His head went jerking back in a shout of laughter. He looked bursting with glee, as if the bounty man had said just the funniest thing.

It startled the bounty man — perhaps that's why Louen did it. After an insult like the bounty man's a fellar could expect his opponent to go reaching for his guns, but — well, not laugh uproariously like this.

The wild, hooting laughter threw the big puncher off his balance mentally — just for a fraction of a second. Louen's hand made a fast white blur as it snaked down for his right Colt, his left hand flung back into the air to give him balance for the throw.

The big puncher saw it clearing leather. No man could match against that, no man could beat that draw now. But he could move quickly, that bounty man.

Louen had come in close, too close. In his desire to talk the big bounty man down he had lost a little caution there. Now he was going back, to give himself room to swing that Colt, but he didn't go back quite quick enough.

Neither did he reckon for the great reach of the big puncher.

The Sharps began to drop to the ground. Before it was there the bounty man's hands had bunched over, that part-drawn gun. It came out, firing, scattering the crowd in a wild, uproarious panic. But the gun wasn't pointing at the bounty man, didn't harm him. And it didn't stay long in Louen's hand.

The bounty man gripped. Loco Lou let go because he had to or have his bones crack under the grip. The Colt dropped.

Then the bounty man, in one sudden, lightning movement, jerked the startled sheriff towards him — jerked, and while the star-decorated body was coming hurtling towards him, the right foot of the bounty man lifted and kicked out.

The shock knocked the breath out of Louen's body and bruised it for days to come. But he hadn't time to think of the shock just then. That driving kick lifted the sheriff off his legs and sent him crashing back against the wall of the Wells Fargo building. Bonnie felt the place shake under the impact.

Then a startled crowd saw the most vicious gunman in Dead End crumple into unconsciousness in the dust of a broken board sidewalk. Kicked into unconsciousness — crazy, killing Jed Louen! For a minute they were dumbfounded, they'd been so sure of the outcome of the impending fight.

The big puncher made matters worse. Insultingly he called:

'I didn't mean to hurt your sher'f that bad. Reckon ef I'd time I'd shore put him to bed!'

Mick Wade woke up and threw a gun. Everyone was so startled they hadn't even seen that big navy Colt that had crept into the bounty man's hand. It barked. Wade's gun, coming up, dropped as he lost most of the knuckles of his gun hand. He reeled back, screaming as he had so often made other men scream.

The sound froze into caution Rope Coltas and Jimmy Maxiil, both about to go for their guns.

The bounty man said:

'You've got right good sense, you galoots. I'm kinda bad at shootin' an I don't reckon to hit a gun hand every time. Could be next time I might perforate some more vulnerable place!'

His voice was soft, ironic, but his manner was formidable.

He crouched out there, the sun throwing a dense black shadow at his feet, his face lost save for the gleam of his eyes, in the shade of his broad brimmed, dust-caked hat. But that Colt was weaving in a menacing circle from one to the other of the crowd that had gone back against the walls at the first sound of shooting. At some time, too, he had picked up his Sharps, and now it was held like a pistol in that powerful left hand of his. The first round could kill a man, even if he couldn't work the pump for the next five in the magazine.

Not a man batted an eyelid. They clung to the sun-baked timbers of the walls, hands instinctively raised to show no offence was intended. And in that moment the one man had the whole town at his mercy.

He snapped:

'Git mounted!' And this time both prisoners jumped to it. They swung up.

The bounty man walked back on to his mount, knocked it into position with quick jabs from his elbows, and then mounted.

They'd been waiting for that moment, waiting to get him for just a second off his guard so that their guns could come streaking into life. But somehow things didn't pan out the way they'd figgered.

The bounty man swung aboard without taking his Colt out of line with their tense, expectant bodies. In one second the moment had passed, the rider was in his saddle — and two Colts were covering them. He'd slipped his Sharps into the saddle boot and come out with the second Colt all in one lightning movement.

His mount was kicked into action

— there was no time for niceties in face of this threatening mob. There were some here who rejoiced to see what had happened to Sheriff Loco Louen, and they might even have been in the majority. But there were many there who identified themselves with the new set up in Dead End, and they were the dangerous people, the killers.

They were edging forward, hands coming inching down. Half of one second of incautious movement and a dozen guns would come flaming into action against the bounty man.

But he was clever. As he sent his mount rearing his guns roared. The nervous, advancing host took the intention to be hostile and directed against themselves, and they went scattering again, flinging themselves into cover and down in the grey dust.

But the bullets were aimed towards the rows of horses hitched in front of the saloon. The deafening roar sent them into a panic, rearing and getting tangled in their harness. If there was to be pursuit, then it was going to be a few seconds at least before any man could get his horse out — and seconds could mean life or death to the bounty man.

He pulled his horse round in that same moment of firing. The mounts of his two prisoners had jumped into stride away down the street, and he started to follow.

Then came the yellow flash as coins were flung in the general direction of Kurt Reimer's livery, stable.

'Ef that ain't enough fer these nags,' they heard the bounty man shout, 'then it oughta be!'

It was that last gesture that set the seal on any reputation the bounty man was to enjoy locally thereafter — that in the face of such danger he could think of Kurt Reimer and even make a faint jest about his horses.

Kurt picked up the gold quickly, then saw Bonnie up in the shadows and limped across to her. She was watching the galloping horses.

Kurt stood by her side and looked in

to the receding cloud of dust. He said softly, so that no one else could hear, 'Ef I'd known I'd haff given that man the best hosses in mein stable!'

He looked at the huddled, dazed figure of Sheriff Louen, crumpled against the wall beneath them, and there was satisfaction on his fat German face.

Bonnie followed the look, then suddenly she gripped Kurt's arm.

'That's the man,' she whispered. 'That's the man to lead us against the Laramie mob!'

5

The Stage Coach Trail

There was frantic confusion out in the street below them now. Kurt had to wait until his voice could be heard.

Men were shouting, cursing, pitching into the terrified, struggling horses. One chestnut gelding got tied up with the head-rope of the long-suffering prospector's mule, and it threw him on to his back where he threshed out madly. The stirring Jed Louen was close to its hoofs, but Jimmy Maxill got across in time and dragged him by the shirt collar into safety.

It took half a minute before the first man had got to his horse, untied it and pulled it out to where it was safe to mount. He hung back, waiting for company. It didn't look healthy, tackling that big *hombre* alone.

So it was that the bounty man got the better part of a minute's lead. Bonnie shrewdly thought, 'He'll need it. His prisoners won't put spurs to their horses.'

As the sheriff's party reared and bucked their horses down the street, fighting to quieten and control them, she heard Kurt say:

'Der bounty man? They don't fight on der side of law and order. But he iss a man, *mein gott* yess, that he iss!'

Bonnie wheeled. Her blue eyes were suddenly blazing.

'It's a chance, Kurt. Give me your fastest horse. I'm going after him, to see if he'll take our side in this battle.'

Kurt blinked in the sunlight, aghast.

He looked after the savage, spurring cowboys, hard on the heels of the bounty man and his prisoners. 'It iss too dangerous,' he protested. 'They would kill you, those Laramie men.'

Bonnie didn't say anything to that. She ran down to Alf York's, grabbed her gun and belt from the hook in the kitchen, then raced out before Mrs York had time to say anything.

Kurt hadn't moved. He didn't think Bonnie Hayday would be mad enough to try to ride through a posse of vengeful gunnies, so he hadn't gone to saddle the horse as she had requested.

She came into the stable the back way. Kurt never saw her because he was watching Sheriff Jed Louen come to consciousness and it was a pleasing sight.

Louen was sick with pain, but he stood up, and after a short while threw off the supporting hands. His face was white, but the smile unexpectedly came to his lips. They saw the flash of white teeth; then Kurt heard him say, 'I'll kill that *hombre* before the sun sets.'

The way he said it, he didn't intend to make a clean kill of it, either. Jed Louen intended that the bounty man should die slowly, over a long period of time, and should be in pain all the while death was coming to him. If anyone had any doubts before, watching Jed Louen now must have settled them.

The man they had put over them to represent law and order in Dead End was as crazy as a horse that had eaten a bagful of loco weed.

Bonnie took the best horse she could see in the stable. Her own was all right, but it had been ridden hard for three days and didn't have any speed, anyway. She knew Kurt wouldn't mind.

She came riding out of the livery stable with her heels already digging for speed. She got it.

It was a big bay gelding, and her light weight seemed to make no difference to it.

As it stretched out into a long, raking stride its broad back seemed to roll like the deck of a ship beneath her. It seemed the very essence of power, hurtling like a thunderbolt along the dusty, rutted trail.

Almost as soon as she began the race she knew she could catch the men ahead. Five minutes later, bursting out from some scrub, she saw the dust cloud across the mesquite and knew it for the posse. They were already shooting.

She seemed to come up to them very quickly. The big puncher was hitting back at his pursuers. He had his hands full watching the two prisoners, but all the same he found time to bring that Sharps into action, and that kept the posse momentarily at a distance.

Bonnie rode right into the tail of the posse, knowing no one would look at her and recognize her. Someone was shouting to the posse to fan out. It sounded like Nils Perhof, the gambler, who would be in on such a chase for the fun of it, and not because he had any affection for the crazy Dead End sheriff.

'Some of you cut ahead and hold the trail agen him,' Bonnie heard him shout.

She stood up in her stirrups. Here the open mesquite rose into the abrupt bluffs fronting the Edwards Plateau, and the trail plunged into a natural cutting before gaining the plain on top. The bounty man was driving his prisoners into the rocky cutting, and for the moment had command of the situation. But the ground on either side of the trail was broken by dried watercourses, and Nils Perhof's idea was to get his men up these rocky pathways in a circling movement that would take them out on to the plains ahead of the bounty hunter and his prisoners.

What was more, Bonnie could see that success would greet the manoeuvre for, with freedom so near, the prisoners were holding back as hard as they could — or dare. The big bounty man wasn't making the pace he needed to win this race.

Bonnie galloped forward, trying to figure out a plan of action, but for the moment nothing came into her alert young mind. She saw half a dozen men go plunging up a promising cleft east of the cutting. By the way they went it seemed hard going but not impossible. The rest of the posse pressed the lone fighter as hard as they dared.

He was in the entrance to the cutting now, his prisoners riding disconsolately twenty yards ahead. He wheeled his mount yet again, and the Sharps spanged lead twice out towards the scattered, close-pressing posse. Twice — that suggested he was running short of ammunition.

Bonnie saw a horse rear, and got an idea that at least one of the shots had found a target. But there were a lot of targets for one lone man to shoot against . . .

She saw him turn swiftly as one of the prisoners began to ride away quickly; he shouted, and sullenly the man brought his horse down to an easier pace. That was the trouble with the prisoners — mostly they hung back, keeping the pace as slow as they dared, but ever anon they would spur quickly, so that the bounty man had always to be on the alert, otherwise he stood a chance of losing at least one of his men.

Bonnie thought: 'He could do something if he didn't have to watch those prisoners.'

She looked up. There was a cloud of dust mushrooming far back beyond the rocky pass, somewhere out on the plain. Too far back to come from any of the hard-riding posse, intent on cutting the big puncher off. She stared at it, wondering what it could mean, but no answers came.

Then suddenly she saw how she could help the bounty man. It wasn't really that an idea came to her — the opportunity suddenly opened up so that she could hardly do anything but take it.

As the bounty man spurred out of sight up the cutting behind his reluctant prisoners, the posse down on the mesquite came riding in towards each other. But now they were no longer pressing hard behind him — they didn't seem in any hurry to ride into the defile.

Bonnie, cantering steadily forward, figured it all out. There was no sense in going fighting up that cutting when within minutes, perhaps, the encircling party would get into position across the trail and either ambush the bounty man or trap him. Respecting the accurate fire of that Sharps rifle, this bunch of cowboys were more inclined to follow into the cutting with caution and at some leisure.

So they were riding slowly together, grouping around a tall, hatless, blond-haired man who could only be Nils Perhof, the gambler.

The way into the cutting was open. Bonnie dug spurs into that mighty-striding horse and streaked into it before anyone knew what was happening.

Thundering up the rock-walled trail, Bonnie sat back on her horse, riding as high as she could. That way she made a bigger target, but she wanted the bounty man to see it was a woman who rode so closely on his trail. She had an idea that, unlike Jed Louen and his friends, the bounty man would be a respecter of women.

Afterwards she wondered why she should think so. Bounty men didn't usually rate any higher than Jed Louen's kind.

She pushed back her hat so that it fell on to her shoulders, bouncing there only because of the strap that came round her throat. Her hair fluttered out in the breeze of their thunderous passage, and she felt that in it lay her chances of safety.

It nearly failed her. She caught up with the bounty man a mile up the cutting. He was having trouble with the prisoners, who were first trying to beat him round the bends, and then were halting across the track and making their horses behave awkwardly.

When she came round that last bend before reaching the trio, he was already waiting for her, rifle hard against his shoulder. A bullet flamed out of the barrel, but even as he triggered he caught the swirl of feminine hair and it deflected his aim.

Bonnie heard the bullet whee-ee-ee-ee into space off the rock wall behind her. In an instant she had both hands in the air and her young, fresh voice was shouting: 'Hold it, mister, you got a friend!'

He held it, though he was plainly suspicious of a trap. Recklessly Bonnie spurred up to him. As she came near enough for him to see her face, the rifle started to come down. There wasn't much guile about Bonnie Hayday.

He sat round watching the two suspicious, alert prisoners, but he could see Bonnie out of the corners of his hard, grey eyes, too.

'What do you want?' he rapped.

Bonnie got his confidence the simplest way. 'That sher'f you kicked over back in Dead End. He killed my grandfather only this week,' she said simply.

He looked at her fully once more after that, nodded slightly, and thereafter gave his complete attention to his prisoners. Bonnie felt that she had been accepted if not as a friend, at least not as a threat to his safety.

Back down the cutting came the ring of hoofs upon rock. The bounty man called, 'Git going,' and the two sullen prisoners kicked their mounts into movement. When they were moving he shouted, 'Faster,' and there was such threat in his voice that instinctively they complied with the order.

Bonnie travelled easily by his side.

'This ain't no good,' she said, and as always when she was excited, she fell into the local way of speech — the speech she had learned during her life among cowboys.

'Why?' came the question, but he didn't take his eyes off the men in front.

'They sent a party up a broken trail to get ahead,' she told him. 'Guess they'll race us, the speed we're goin'.'

He asked: 'What's the best way out of

the fix? You know this country?'

'Like anything,' she retorted laconically. 'You've got a rifle, brother, and none of the posse's carryin' more than Colts. If you could make the open ground ahead of 'em, you could hold 'em back till kingdom come with that Sharps.'

'I'm not running away from my prisoners.' His voice was harsh.

'I don't want you to. I'll bring 'em up for you, and you can cover us with your rifle.'

He was startled, seemed perturbed. 'A girl couldn't handle these snakes,' he said roughly.

'No? This girl lost a fine grandparent this week. If they turned on me, why, I guess I'd blow an arm off 'em and feel good about it.'

The bounty man called:

'You, Dutch George, and you, King — you heard what this girl said?' King Rattler didn't turn, but Dutch George's blue-scrub chin came round in a brief, hard nod. He'd heard, all right.

The bounty man spoke softly:

'I want these galoots alive, but don't you take no chances, gal. Ef they git too close, drill holes in thar heads.' He checked, just as he was starting to spur away. Looked at her, his eyes sharp points of grey light in the powder-mask of a face. 'Your name, gal? I'd like . . . to know it, I reckon.'

'Bonnie Hayday,' she flashed. 'And yours?'

'Tom M'Grea.' His hand came down on top of her slim brown one — just a quick, comradely touch. 'Good shootin', Bonnie.'

'Good ridin', cowboy,' she yelled, as his horse leaned to round the overhanging rock wall. 'You'll make it!' She had a feeling he might just do it; that entry the posse had gone up had looked rough going and would be slow.

Dutch George pulled rein. He snarled, 'I ain't goin' no farther.' King Rattler let his horse take a dozen more steps before drawing rein and sitting round to watch the showdown.

Bonnie was prepared for it. Her gun pointed above Dutch George's shapeless hat. Quite clearly her voice rang out:

'I'll give you two chances to change your mind. You won't get a third, Dutch George. My first bullet will go a foot over your head.'

She pulled trigger. A heavy round bullet smacked itself flat against the unyielding rock a foot above Dutch George's head. The scrub-face flinched and ducked involuntarily.

'Your next chance will leave you without a hat,' continued Bonnie calmly. Her Colt exploded. Dutch George's hat leapt away into the hardy chaparral — and he lost some hair in the process.

'That was your last chance. Start movin', critter, because the next bullet says it's goin' to put that ugly nose of yours right through your thick skull!'

She wasn't bluffing. She couldn't bluff against two men as vicious as these. If he tried to defy her, she would have to kill him if only to protect herself. The picture of old Silver Sam Hayday rose before her mind to give her the courage for such a deed.

But it wasn't needed. Dutch George's nerve broke. He spat viciously, suddenly, then gave in, and started his mount at a fast trot up the winding trail. King Rattler didn't need any demonstrations of strength: he kept steadily ahead of the raging, quietly cursing Dutch George. But his eyes were bleak; given a chance it would go hard with the girl riding on their heels.

Another mile up the valley and suddenly lead came spanging past her ear. She turned, groaning to herself.

The rest of the posse must have come riding into the cutting after her, and they'd gained during the various altercations — they'd been coming up quickly and quietly all the time, and now they were within Colt range.

She let rip with a quick shot back over her shoulder, but she knew that firing that way she could do little harm.

Now the advantage lay with the posse, because they were firing as they came — she was having to turn and fire while on the retreat.

She shouted to the prisoners:

'Go your darndest!' They didn't increase their pace. She shouted desperately, 'OK, if that's how you want it I'll shoot one of you and take the other through alone. Make up your minds which it's to be!'

King Rattler immediately struck spurs to his horse and went plunging round a bend. Dutch George gave a hoarse bellow and shot after him. Dutch George wasn't risking any lead because he was behind-man to his companion. The quick-witted girl's ruse had worked. For the moment they were making a pace that kept them clear of their pursuers.

They were riding up boldly now, realizing they were only faced by a girl armed not with a Sharps rifle but with the much shorter-ranged Colt. Bonnie heard their loud, triumphant 'Yippees!'

and threw lead back, but it didn't stop them.

Madly she urged on the two flagging horses ahead; her own wasn't bothered in the least by her lighter weight. If she had wanted she could have deserted the prisoners and raced on to safety ahead of the posse, but something of the bounty man's tenacity had entered in her — she vowed to herself that not for anything would she let go her hold over the ruffianly pair.

Those pounding hooves were nearer now, a lot nearer. They weren't shooting, probably recognizing her and wanting to take her alive. She heard voices — so close she recognized some. They were as near as all that, but she didn't despair, didn't give up hope.

She knew they were nearly out of the cutting now, nearly up on to the open plain. At any time she expected to hear the vicious crack of the Sharps ahead of her. When that came she knew she would be safe, because no man would dare emerge from that narrow defile with a Sharps covering it.

When she did hear the Sharps, though, it wasn't being fired to help her. Over the noise of the pursuit she heard quite clearly three swift rifle shots away up ahead. She guessed immediately the import of them. Big Tom M'Grea was holed up somewhere ahead, fighting back against those other posse men who had gone to get ahead and trap him.

Madly she urged the horses along now. She couldn't be far from the bounty man, his rifle — and possible safety. But as she rode the thought hammered in her brain, 'Did Big M'Grea win the race?'

For if the posse had won, then she would find the bounty man stuck in the cutting, trapped as they had intended to trap him — and with this mob close behind.

They swept out of the narrow defile so quickly that before they knew what they were doing they were riding on the more level trail of the plain beyond.

And Big M'Grea was lying out there, lying up on a knoll which let him look down the first rolling surfaces of the bluff that fell so sheerly aftwards down on to the Neuces plain below. Not very high, that knoll, but it was sufficient to give him command of the cutting up which Bonnie and the two prisoners came pounding, as well as the broken way quarter of a mile east of it in which the six posse men were holed up.

Bonnie let rip with a cheer, 'Yip-yipyippee-ee-ee!'

M'Grea saw riders close behind. He had only two rounds left in his rifle. He gave them both — quickly — to Bonnie's pursuers. A cowboy from the Laramie ranch stopped thinking of the bonus he'd get from the boss for this little shindig. He wouldn't draw a bonus this side of the Long Trail ever again. The second shot put Nils Perhof's mount down with a bullet through the skull.

It stopped the posse, just as it had stopped those first riders up the broken gully. Bonnie came wheeling round the knoll, shepherding her prisoners before her. The grim, powder-grey giant of a bounty man rose and loped down to his own horse, but as he ran he was looking at this girl who had come so unexpectedly out of the blue to help him — and help him she had, indeed.

He was thinking:

'She's too nice to be mixed up in this sort of business. It ain't right I should endanger her.'

The bounty man swung into his saddle. Bonnie's eyes narrowed. 'Reckon you'd better lie holed up for half an hour an' keep that posse safe in the gulch,' she said. She was thinking they'd need half an hour's lead, with two unco-operative prisoners.

He shook his head wrily. When he spoke his voice came softly, so that the men ahead couldn't hear.

'I can't hold no one in any gulch. For why?' He patted the butt of his trusty Sharps. 'This hyar rifle opines not to work no more till she gets somep'n in her belly.'

'You're out of ammunition?' A gasp of dismay came from the girl.

'Just that. I gave you my last two shots. But I guess you don't need to tell my pards ahead,' he said cynically, with a nod to the brooding backs of his prisoners.

'Oh, dear,' sighed Bonnie. 'Just when I thought we stood a chance.' She looked back. They were riding in the lee of the knoll, and so far none of the posse had ventured out.

He divined her thoughts. 'They won't come out in a hurry — which is to our advantage, of course. They'll reckon maybe I'm sittin' waitin' fer 'em with my Sharps. But when nothin' happens, they'll get ter stickin' hats up on sticks, an' when they don't lose 'em they'll get around to the right answers. They'll maybe let us get five minutes' start, mebbe ten. But I don't reckon no more.'

Bonnie dug heels into her mount and brought it up behind the prisoners.

'Git goin' you ornery cayuses,' she shouted. 'Make time, darn you — make time!'

They went careering away as she slapped her hat over their haunches, and the grey eyes of the big bounty man gleamed with humour.

'That shore is some gal,' he said to himself. 'Now, what have I done to deserve help from such a gal, huh?'

It didn't occur to him that the help he got was incidental. Bonnie Hayday wanted him — the bounty hunter. This seemed the only way of keeping her prize out of the hands of the posse and alive.

At which moment Bonnie pulled hard on her reins. Ahead of them was a big mushroom of dust cloud — far bigger than when she had seen it from the plain below. They were nearly upon it now.

The bounty man looked at Bonnie, but she shook her head. She didn't understand it. Then he glanced quickly back over his shoulder, and Bonnie said: 'It's pretty hopeless, isn't it? Even if we do get ten minutes start — '

They rode forward towards that advancing dust cloud. Big M'Grea's caked lips cracked open and she heard him mutter, 'So near, darn it. All this way an' then to go bust on the last hundred miles.'

'You're thinking of the reward?' Bonnie's eyes were fixed on the yellow cloud ahead. Now she began to hear a faint rumbling sound.

'Shore, what else?' Back he looked again, but still there was no sign of their pursuers advancing out on to the plain. They'd got a two-minute lead, whatever that advancing dust cloud portended.

Bonnie kept her eyes forward. 'They'll be after us any time. If they catch up on us and you see it's hopeless, will you do something for me — something pretty big for a boun — ' She stopped quickly.

Ironically he asked, 'Fer a bounty man, were you goin' to say?' He nodded. 'Shore, I know what opinion

120

people have about bounty men.'

That rolling noise was growing louder. Any moment now they might see the cause of it over the rolling undulations that obscured the trail ahead.

'Is it a fair one?' she flashed.

He considered. Then, 'Reckon so,' he said, and she sighed. She didn't want to think of Big M'Grea as a callous, conscienceless manhunter, a man who lived by the rewards offered for bringing men — even bad men — in to die.

She heard his voice. 'You didn't say what you wanted me ter do, Bonnie?'

'I want you to keep alive. If they get too near, ride for it. Circle round and get back into Dead End after dark. Go to Kurt Reimer — he's the man who sold you these horses. Tell him Bonnie Hayday says you're the man for the job. He'll look after you.'

'An' the job?'

'Leading the good but timid citizens in a fight for their existence against the crooks and gamblers who are in complete control over the whole area.'

M'Grea said wearily, 'It doesn't seem a job fer me.'

'But it's logical.' Bonnie turned in her saddle. 'You're an unofficial representative of the law — you're the instrument of the law even if you do it only for — '

'For blood money?' His face was quite impassive under that grey dust layer on his cheeks.

'For the rewards offered. All right, why not make the law your job? Help clean up the crooks in Dead End, and there's a nice new office waiting for you, with a good salary attached.'

'Office?'

'The sheriff's office.'

'I see.' That noise was growing thunderous over the vast silence of the plain. Then his head shook obstinately. 'I can't think of anything else until these men are handed over to the sheriff of Stampede. I've trailed 'em to California, an' I've rustled 'em all the way back. I've nearly lost 'em a hundred times, but by the sacred mule I'm gonna stick tight to 'em right to the end of the trail!'

Bonnie felt a thrill as she heard his low, growling voice utter that determined resolve. He was a man, this M'Grea, a fighting man.

But it didn't suit her. 'The posse behind — '

He looked back. They must still be lying doggo in the broken land, thinking he was waiting for them with his long-range Sharps.

'I'll beat 'em yet,' he vowed, and seeing his hard, jutting jaw she had a feeling that though the odds seemed hopeless against him, he would win through because he simply didn't know when he was beaten. And she wondered how many times he had been in similar situations on the long trail back from California.

Abruptly, eyes watching that yellow cloud over the next rise, he said, 'You're right about 'em catching up with us

— even if we get ten minutes' lead. They're bound to do it — ef we stick to the trail. They've faster hosses than we have, and my prisoners will find one way or another of slowing the pace.'

'So?'

'So I'm aimin' to turn off the trail just as soon as we come to a hard patch where they'll miss any slight hoof-prints.' He looked at the soft soil of the prairie — it didn't look very stony hereabouts.

Bonnie thought rapidly, then said, 'There's a gully sweeps across the trail half a mile ahead. They can't use this trail most of the winter because of it.'

'We'll turn off there,' M'Grea said then got out both Colts as they heard pounding hoofs ahead.

He started to say, 'Give us ten minutes' start so that we can get lost somewhere out there and we'll lick 'em yet.'

But Bonnie interrupted. 'We'll get no ten minutes' start. Look what's coming

— the once-a-week stage coach to Dead End!'

She'd forgotten about that, but it completely upset their calculations now.

6

Bonnie Rides Alone

They drew rein impulsively to await the arrival of the coach. It was coming along at a fair lick, swaying because of the rough trail, the four horses kicking up a cloud of dust that must have made life almost unendurable for the occupants of the Wells Fargo coach behind.

For once Big M'Grea was slow to grasp the significance of the approaching coach. 'I don't understand — '

'When that coach goes into the cutting the posse'll shout and ask the driver where we are. He'll tell 'em he's seen us back down the trail a piece and then they'll come a r'arin' after us.'

M'Grea nodded. 'Looks like I'd better hold up a stage coach, then,' he said softly. 'Ef that's the only way.'

'While I get a lead with the boys?' He

nodded. Bonnie shook her head. 'You hold up this coach for any reason and automatically you become an outlaw with a price on your head. Wells Fargo don't let people go around stickin' up their coaches.'

M'Grea swore with sudden, unexpected passion — 'After all I've gone through, I'll turn outlaw ef it gets me through to Stampede with my men!'

'And afterwards?' The coach driver was standing on his big footbrake, bracing back against the long reins to the leaders. His shouting brought heads to the coach windows. The tyre blocks screamed against the warm steel, the wheels locked and skidded through the dust, but the coach slowed and then stopped.

'Afterwards can wait,' M'Grea said roughly. He started to go forward, then Bonnie spurred a pace ahead.

'You take the prisoners. Turn off at the gulch and I'll come on after you. I'm going to stay and hold up the coach, only not with a gun.'

She rode up to the driver. Big M'Grea sat hunched in his saddle, watching and thinking, and then he shrugged, accepting her plan, and ordered his prisoners to keep right on past the coach.

The driver looked curiously at the three men, as did the passengers at the windows, but M'Grea just nodded briefly and rode through. Bonnie came up and took hold of the sweating nearside horse. It seemed a careless gesture, but a man can't whip up a horse while a girl is holding and patting it.

The driver called down gruffly, 'Anythin' I c'n do fer you, Miss Hayday?' She didn't know the man, but he seemed to recognize her. She considered. M'Grea was loping quickly out of sight over the next brow.

She began to talk, asking about her foreman — making it sound as though he was late in and could have had an accident on the trail — especially, that bit back where it skirted the soft sand which could suck a horse and rider up in less than ten minutes — five if you struggled.

The driver and a couple of cowboys riding up top debated the matter. No, they hadn't seen no trace, miss. Sure, they hadn't been particularly noticin', but they opined they'd have seen something if a rider had been on that trail just before them.

Bonnie kept them talking. The driver at first didn't seem to mind being stopped, probably being quite willing to give his panting horses a chance to get their breath, but after a few minutes one of the passengers took a hand.

He came swinging down on to the trail — an Easterner if ever she'd seen one. He wore fancy riding pants, with leggings that had been highly polished at the start of the journey but had suffered on the way down. He was a biggish man, spare, but he looked lean and hard and as tough as they came.

The Easterner didn't seem to have such respect for girlhood as the Texans.

He rapped, nasally, Yankee-fashion, 'Ain't this coach gonna move agen ter-day? What're we stopped for?'

The driver called down: 'It's Miss Hayday. She's kinda worried about her foreman.'

Bonnie gave a quick, covert glance backwards. Still the posse hadn't ventured from cover. It must have been all of seven or eight minutes since they started off from the knoll. Her heart bumped painfully with suppressed excitement. They might, after all, steal a march on the posse and get away. Desperately she played for more time, and fortunately mention of her name seemed to have an effect upon the Easterner.

'Hayday?' His hand dived into the inside pocket of his smart-cut, tweed riding-jacket: It came out with a red leather-bound book that might have been a diary, and he turned a few pages then looked up quickly at Bonnie. His face tried to smile now, but he thought she preferred it in its normal unsmiling toughness: Some faces just aren't made for smiles.

'Your father owns the Hayday ranch along the river bed, eh?'

'Nope.' Bonnie was emphatic. 'I own it. It was my grandfather's, only a snake came an' bit him last week an' he died. Now I'm the boss.'

The Easterner began to smile in a big, friendly way. He stuck up his hand to Bonnie. 'I'm right glad to meet you, Miss Hayday,' he said. 'I intended looking up the boss of the Hayday ranch; now it'll be a pleasure, comin' out to see you.'

'Comin' out to see me?' Bonnie was startled. She couldn't understand why any Easterner might want to come to see her, Bonnie Hayday — why the name of Hayday should be in such an impressive diary. She knew instinctively it had nothing to do with her relatives back East — then what could it mean?

She never had time to ask him. The driver was staring ahead down the trail: she heard him growl: 'Looks like we got more company!'

Startled, Bonnie flashed a glance back along the trail. Silhouetted against the sear-yellow scrub of the knoll was a group of horsemen.

The posse!

They must have worked their way out of the broken country and discovered the trick that had been played on them.

Bonnie dug heels into her horse and sent it plunging headlong up the trail. She heard startled exclamations from the coach passengers, and her departure was so abrupt that it nearly knocked the Easterner down into the dust, but she hadn't time for apologies or explanations.

Far behind her she heard a cry as the posse took up the chase, but she smiled with satisfaction even so. She knew they wouldn't catch her on this long-striding horse, and holding up the stage coach like that must have added minutes to the lead that M'Grea had with his prisoners.

When she reached the gully that cut

right across the trail — an awkward place for a lumbering stage coach to negotiate — she pulled her willing horse into it and let it scramble up the stony track. Within a minute she knew she was out of sight of the trail behind, and she let her horse go more easily. The chances were that the posse would go blinding hell-for-leather past the gully end, and would only think of it when they began to realize that their quarry wasn't riding ahead. Then they'd hunt for tracks and come back to the place where they'd turned off.

But that could take time. Perhaps so much time that the posse would give up the chase in disgust. Perspiring as she clung to the saddle, Bonnie thought it was hot enough to make anyone want to give up riding around in the sun.

M'Grea must have been pushing his prisoners hard, for it took Bonnie half an hour to catch up with them. They were still traversing the rolling prairie under cover of the dried water course, but the way was getting too stony for comfort. When Bonnie caught up with the bounty hunter he was about to climb up on to the softer land and risk being seen.

Bonnie called softly, 'Hallo, there, big feller,' and the three men ahead reined and sat waiting. The horses stood with heads drooping, blowing hard through their nostrils and quivering after their exertions in the hot noonday sun. They were in much worse condition than Bonnie's bay.

M'Grea's face seemed to go less hard at sight of her. 'I was worrying,' he said simply. 'I don't feel I oughta get a gal to risk anythin' fer me.'

Bonnie took time off to get her hat back on her head. The glare from the near-desert was intolerable now that the sun was riding overhead.

'I'm wantin' you for my own reasons, Tom.' she told him. 'I don't give a hang about your bounty prizes; there's more important work for a fellow like you back in Dead End.'

'So you were saying.' He put his

horse to the steep slope of the gulch and rode out of it. On top he turned and gestured with his empty Sharps and because they didn't yet know it was without menace the two prisoners wearily followed up after him. The bay went climbing up on its own, eager for more work. Bonnie wondered how much Kurt would take for the beast — it was a horse worth having.

On top they all paused to look round, but the broad, undulating prairie seemed devoid of life.

'Looks like we shook 'em off, thanks to the lead you gave me,' said M'Grea after a while. 'Reckon we c'n take it steady now.' His eyes trailed from the back depths where Dead End lay hidden and lifted to meet hers. 'Maybe that's the last of the trouble I'm goin' ter get.'

Bonnie brought her eyes back to his — blue eyes meeting grey. 'Mebbe,' she said. 'But mebbe your trouble's just beginning. Take a look at that smoke in the sky and tell me what it reads!'

He came upright with a jerk. Far north, where the Brazos river would lie, three broken spirals of smoke rose thin but clear into the blue Texas sky. Further north still, but east of it, was a lone answering smoke.

'Comanches?' she asked.

He shook his head. 'At a guess I'd say Apaches.' He watched the smoke signals through narrowed eyes for a moment. 'I'd say they're holin' up, hopin' the Comanches won't chase 'em so far.' He shrugged. 'What's the difference, though, between one Injun or another? Comanche or Apache — they shore like the hair of the white man, I reckon.'

'And that's the way you have to go?'

'Pretty near. A mite east of it, but a whole lot too close to be comfortable.' He spoke flatly, without emotion in his voice, and she wondered what was going through his mind now. It must have been galling to find, almost within sight of his goal, that another and very threatening obstacle was in his path.

'You'll go through, though?' Her blue eyes searched his for an answer. She didn't know what to hope.

'Shore. I'll go through with my prizes even though the whole Indian nation is waitin' fer me.' It was as though every hardship merely added to his obstinacy; and yet just then Bonnie began to feel another emotion — that of hatred.

It was as though the bounty man cherished deep within him a hatred of his prisoners that was sufficient to make him go even to his death rather than lose them. Bounty men were new to Bonnie, and she wondered if this always happened — if bounty men developed a hatred of the men they brought in, because of necessity the work entailed great hardship and danger for them.

'So you won't come back with me and help fight the Laramie outfit?'

'Mebbe another day,' he said mechanically. She had a feeling he wasn't quite listening to her, hadn't ever listened to what she was saying, so intent was he on this mission that had taken him already over two thousand hard, dangerous miles.

'When you've got rid of your prisoners you might come back to Dead End?' Hopefully she clung to the straw.

'Mebbe.' He was still looking at those smoke signals. 'But I guess it'll be some time before I do that. There's work fer me to do — guess thar's a lot of work fer me piled up an' waitin' back in Stampede. That's got to be attended to first,' he ended doggedly.

'I see,' whispered Bonnie. That sounded like more bounties. Maybe Stampede had other men for the bounty man to go out and track down.

'Is it worth it — months of travelling and fighting just to get five hundred dollars?' she asked suddenly.

His face grew hard.

'In this case, ma'am,' he said, and she noticed the deliberate politeness of his speech, 'it is well worth it.'

He rode away, picking out an easy trail through the mesquite. She thought: 'He expects me to follow, to help him bring his men in.' But that wasn't part of her plan. She wanted to bring *him* back, the prisoners were no concern of hers.

The Rattler inched towards her. Her gun came out of its holster just as quick as most men could throw it.

'Hold your distance!' she rapped.

The Rattler's quick, evil little eyes were fixed on M'Grea, a dozen yards ahead. His voice came soft and only loud enough for her to hear. It was a desperate, rather clumsy suggestion that he put up.

'You want M'Grea to help you, huh? OK, give us a break. Let us get a lead of a hundred yards, and he'll never catch us on that tired hoss of his.'

He turned his head towards her, and perhaps that was a mistake he made, because few people could look on that shrunken, vicious little face and feel amiable towards it.

'Ef we get away, mebbe he'll feel like takin' a job with you, miss,' he whispered cunningly.

For one moment, because her despair had been so acute, she was tempted. It would have been so easy. She knew that rifle was an empty bluff, and she knew she could ride close in and slam a gun in M'Grea's ribs before he knew what was happening.

If she wanted she could permit these prisoners to escape. And then what?

She relaxed, the temptation passing like a receding wind through the mesquite. She couldn't do it, not on big Tom M'Grea. It would have been too cruel to have wrested his prizes away from him right when victory was so near at hand. Besides, she could only do it because he trusted her, and she wasn't the kind to play false to a trust.

M'Grea was no fool. He came wheeling round suddenly, called as they came up: 'I heard the Rattler spillin' pisen. What was he sayin', Bonnie?'

Bonnie shrugged.

'He was just wantin' me to stick you up an' let them get away. He reckoned I might get you to go with me then,' she ended bitterly.

'But you turned him down?' M'Grea's voice was soft; he was watching her calculatingly.

She nodded, her hair dropping before her face in a lovely soft mass as her head came forward.

'I don't doublecross,' she said coldly, and at that he said: 'I reckon you don't, Bonnie. I saw that first time I looked at you.'

And it sounded like a deep and sincere compliment, the way he said it — so unexpectedly sincere that it brought a wave of warmth into Bonnie's cheeks.

She felt her heart fluttering a little, and she told herself this was silly — you didn't get to botherin' about the opinion of bounty men.

But she was, and she realized it. Big M'Grea was too much of a man not to be attractive to a girl.

M'Grea nodded.

'You have my thanks fer not listenin'

ter this skunk,' he said, and the Rattler went forward with a savage scowl at Bonnie. 'Well, let's git movin'.'

The three men started away. When M'Grea wanted to speak to Bonnie he found she was not at his side. He looked round. She was sitting her horse on top of the gulch, not moving, drooping in the saddle, despondent. She looked very small on top of that giant beast, suddenly very frail.

M'Grea called a halt, then came back towards Bonnie.

'You not comin', Bonnie?' he asked.

'Why should I? I'm not interested in your prisoners — or the bounty they'll bring!'

That last part of her sentence was bitter, the bitterness that comes with the understanding of defeat.

'No, I guess not.' He sat there, saying no more. She wondered if bounty men had any susceptible feelings, they winced inwardly when they heard the contempt in other people's voices.

'I'm goin' back. I shouldn't have

come after you. It wasn't to be expected that you would forget what brought you through Dead End, and go back and help us fight those crooks.'

'I didn't ask you to come — '

'I know. I didn't say you did.'

'But I'm glad you came,' he ended softly.

'Sure you're glad.' Bonnie had an unusual feeling that she wanted to hurt someone. 'I saved your bounty for you, didn't I? Maybe you'll remember that when you draw your five hundred dollars.'

'I can remember you without any bounties to remind me,' he said, and it was only afterwards she realized he had said 'you' when she had spoken only of his bounties.

'What are you going to do?' he queried.

'I'm going back to my ranch.' Those lovely blue eyes were sombre, brooding. 'I'm going back to find a man with guts enough to take the war into the enemy's camp.'

'And ef you don't?'

'I'll start the war myself. Yes — me, a girl!'

Then, in the passion of the moment, she flung her horse round and went thundering away south parallel with the gulch. When she looked back she found the trio had disappeared on the prairie.

Far to the north of her those smoke signals poured out their dark messages. She turned, despondent, suddenly fearing for the big man, though he had disappointed her so.

She came into Dead End to find that she, Bonnie Hayday, had been branded a criminal in her absence; and the principal support to the charge came from a man she had met only once in her life — an Easterner who wore dude riding-pants but was no dude.

There was a price on her head for aiding and abetting in the escape of a man who had struck down the law as represented by Sheriff Jed Louen.

'Holy smoke,' Bonnie whispered, 'I'm

an outlaw — me, Bonnie Hayday!'

And surprisingly it tickled her sense of humour, and she felt cheerful for the first time since she had left M'Grea.

7

Wanted by the Law

Bonnie met a lone rider on the edge of Dead End, just in the bottom where the cottonwoods threw a screen to hide the unloveliness of the cowtown.

He took one look at her, straightened in the saddle and looked round, then exclaimed:

'Hell's bells, Miss Hayday, get outa sight off the trail!'

She was a bit alarmed as he started to ride her into the cottonwoods. He was a man she didn't know much more than by sight, and until now she hadn't felt very sure of the fellow. But right at this moment he proved he was straight.

He was a smallholder named Frank M'Cone. He'd just moved in on to a couple of hundred acres that ran west of the Colorado, about fifteen miles out of Dead End. Most people didn't think much of the land, but M'Cone was working hard at fencing it, and seemed tolerably satisfied with his first year's work.

M'Cone must have sensed her doubts, because he started to explain right way.

'Sher'f Louen shore wants to lay his hands on you, Miss Hayday.'

Bonnie came off the road pretty quick at that.

'Louen?'

'Shore, Loco Lou hissel'.'

M'Cone had a bright face when you looked closely at him. He got down off his horse, stiffly because he spent most of his life in the saddle these days. He looked a very dusty, faded sort of man in his worn old clothes, but there was purpose behind his movements.

'What's Louen got against me?' demanded Bonnie, looking down from the great height of her bay. M'Cone had some sacks fixed across his saddle bow — they probably contained supplies for his lonely farm. Laboriously he untied them and let them drop on either side of his horse.

'You helped a fellar to git away, didn't you, miss?'

'A bounty hunter.'

'Shore. They told me about it back in town. The *hombre* up and kicked in Louen's guts, didn't he?' he asked, then apologized for using such a word in the presence of a lady.

Bonnie nodded.

'I saw it happen. I thought Louen would never get up again.'

For a moment she had a vision of Jed Louen, crashing back against the timber wall of the Wells Fargo office, his face a white mask of sudden pain, yet grinning even then with that curious, crazy mirth of his.

'He got up.' M'Cone spat as if he thought that wasn't as good as it might have been. 'I reckon Louen will kill the bounty man of he lays hands on him.'

Bonnie said: 'That bounty man shore is tough. Guess he's as tough as they

148

make 'em along the Brazos, and that's sayin' something.'

'You know where he's headin'?'

Bonnie nodded.

M'Cone was no fool. He thought for a moment, then said:

'Mebbe that's why Louen opins ter git his hands on you. He's plumb crazy, that *hombre*. So crazy he'll kill hissel' ter even scores with the bounty man. Mebbe he reckons to find out from you where the fellar's lit out to.'

'It could be. But he won't find out from me,' said Bonnie determinedly. 'I don't hold for bounty men, as a rule, but I like Jed Louen less than I could like a rattlesnake.'

'Shore.' M'Cone had probably known her grandfather. His voice held quiet sympathy. 'Shore, I know how you feel, miss.'

She started to pull her horse round, but M'Cone caught its head and held it.

'I wouldn't go near Dead End just yet, miss,' he told her quietly. 'They've got things all fixed agen you, in any event.'

'Fixed?' Bonnie wasn't quite understanding the position she was in just yet.

'Shore. That bounty man kicked over the sheriff. OK, that's been made a crime he's got to answer for. Burt Laramie put up a couple of hundred dollars reward for him. The Laramies aim to keep their sher'f good an' strong, I reckon,' he ended grimly.

'They're going to let people see that Jed Louen can't be knocked around by anyone?'

'Shore, that's about it. That in turn makes 'em stronger.' M'Cone spat again. Everyone could see through the Laramies' move to uphold the law in Dead End. 'Waal, Burt heard from the posse that you'd gone on ahead an' helped the bounty man escape. They wasn't sure at first it was really you that lit off past them, but when the coach came in there was a dude Easterner to say you was with the bounty man an' his prisoners. He said you even gave him your name.'

'I did.' Bonnie's brow puckered. She couldn't figure out how this Easterner came to fit into things. Why, for instance, he should have the name of Hayday in that precious, red-leather diary. She dismissed the thought and said: 'So I'm an outlaw, too?'

'Looks like it.' M'Cone sighed. ''Course no one'll take it seriously around hyar, only the Laramie mob. But they'll try'n pull you in, I guess, just to find out what you know about the bounty man.' Significantly he added: 'They might try ter git it out of you, too, miss. Mebbe it wouldn't be pleasant right now, fallin' into their hands.'

Bonnie thought of Loco Lou and shuddered. Mentally she resolved not to fall into his lands. As M'Cone said, it wouldn't be at all nice.

Suddenly she felt helpless, and looked at the hardy smallholder for guidance.

'What am I to do?' she asked.

He had got it all figured out, like the resourceful backwoodsman he was.

'I'd go back East fer a while. That's whar your grandfather shore wanted you ter go, anyway.' He spat. 'This ain't no place fer a gal, not these days round Dead End. I reckon things is shore goin' ter start a-buzzin' any time now.'

'And I intend to be here when they do,' she declared impulsively.

He seemed to ignore the remark, intent as he was on the plans he had made for her.

'I'll ride back into Dead End and let Alf York know you're hid up hyar. He was your grandpappy's best friend, I reckon. I guess he'll take care o' your ranch while you're away, an' give you the money you need right now ter take you back East.'

He climbed painfully, slowly, into his saddle, but once up there he sat like a man who knew how to ride a horse. Bonnie was shaking her head obstinately.

'It's a nice, thoughtful plan, mister, but I'm not leaving this neck of the country until my grandfather's murderer has been brought to justice.'

M'Cone opened his mouth to make a mild protest, then he saw the determined expression on that pretty young face and sighed.

'I know that look,' he said, and there was a dry humour in his voice. 'When that look came into old Silver Sam's face, we knew it was wastin' breath ter argie with him.'

Bonnie's face relaxed into a smile.

'Then you know it's wasting your breath trying to send me out of the county.'

'All right.' M'Cone gathered up the reins. 'All the same, I'll ride back in ter let Alf York know you're hidin' up hyar. Mebbe he'll figger out what's best fer you ter do.'

He walked his horse slowly on to the trail. No one was in sight. He called back: 'Keep outa sight till I return, miss. I wouldn't like anythin' ter happen ter Silver Sam's granddaughter. He shore thought a powerful lot about you.' And then he told her there was food in those sacks, if she felt hungry, touched spurs to his old horse and cantered away.

Bonnie didn't feel hungry, so she left the sacks unopened. She remembered there was a brook somewhere back among the cottonwoods, and she took her horse to water it. It was nearly dry, but she scuffed some of the muck out where it seeped through the ground, and after a few minutes there was enough in the hole to satisfy the gallant bay. She herself went thirsty because the water didn't look too good, and she had forgotten to ask M'Cone if he had a water-bottle.

Then she went back and sat just out of sight of the trail, though she was able to see it if she stood up under the shady cottonwoods.

She was there nearly an hour, and most of the time she was thinking of M'Grea — thinking what bitterness it was to have met the man they needed and yet not be able to enlist his services.

About four in the afternoon she saw someone come riding out of Dead End. As few people were likely to be abroad at that time of day, with the sun just blistering the place, she guessed it would be old Alf York.

It was. For his bulk he had got a horse out of Kurt Reimer's stable that was more used to shafts than a saddle, but it bore him all right.

When he came near she stood up and waved, and he turned his horse across the mesquite towards her. She wondered where Frank M'Cone was, but as Alf hefted himself out of the saddle she saw the smallholder come trotting quickly down the trail a quarter of a mile away. The canny Frank must have held back so as to make sure that Alf wasn't followed out of town.

Alf's heavy face creased into a smile as she ran up to take his hand.

'Hello, hoss-thief!' he said, looking

significantly at the bay. She laughed. 'They hang hoss-thieves in this county,' he added mock-warningly.

'They've got to catch me first,' she retorted. 'Don't you know I'm an outlaw with a price on my head?'

The smile left him then. He sat down heavily in the shade of the cottonwood and mopped his steaming face. Frank came creaking out of his saddle and crossed to join them.

'You got yourself in trouble, Bonnie,' old Alf said. 'You're a gal, but that won't make much difference to the Laramie outfit if they catch you.'

'I don't intend to let them catch me.'

She watched the men share a sack of Bull Durham and roll themselves a smoke each. The horses were grazing under cover, and she felt safe along with these two men.

'But what are your plans?'

So Bonnie told them. She'd had an hour in which to figure them out.

'Some day law's got to come to Dead End. Nothing ever stops the coming of law. We'll get it, just like they've got it back in San Antonio, Austin an' Houston. But it will come all the sooner if we prepare the citizens for it.'

Alf looked weary.

'Shore, shore, I know that. But we've tried, haven't we? You've campaigned all across the county, but you couldn't get men willin' ter set up openly agen the Laramie mob. For the moment they're so strong it'd be suicide to start up agen 'em.'

'But some day someone's got to start.' Bonnie suddenly grabbed his arm. 'Why not start not today, but tonight?'

Alf stopped sifting dry soil through his big, banana-like fingers. 'Tonight?'

'Yes. You said we daren't set up open opposition to the Laramie mob. OK, then let's start doing it secretly. A handful of men operating at night could create havoc with the Laramies.'

Alf stopped smoking and turned to look at Frank M'Cone.

Bonnie urged: 'They've hustled our

beef, they've bust our fences, turned cattle into crops, and shot up our riders. There's terror over the land — terror and death. My grandfather was shot early this week, last night someone stampeded two hundred beeves of Alec Stewart's into a ravine. Next week someone else will suffer or get hurt. How much longer are we to sit idle without trying to hit back? Oh, I know we've no direct proof that this is all the work of the Laramie brothers, but there's no one got a shadow of doubt in their own minds that it is. Why, for weeks now the people in the valley bottom have been — '

Suddenly she stopped speaking, letting the vowel sound of the last word trail for seconds. Her intelligent young face lifted, looked at the two men intently.

'That's queer,' she said. 'You know, I haven't thought of that before.'

'Thought of what?' Alf York was alert, knowing from past experience this girl to have a tidy-sized brain.

'Why, that all the damage is being done to ranches in the valley bottom. It suddenly came to me — I've never thought of it before. Doesn't it strike you as curious that people just a way up the hillsides don't suffer at all, only us people alongside the river?'

Alf let his big hand fall in a great slap across his fat thigh.

'Doggone it, I never noticed it, either. Now, that is queer, just as you say. But — what does it add up to, Bonnie? Can you figger it out?'

Her head shook.

'Not yet. But it looks to me it might be a good thing if it was figgered out. I always felt that the Laramies were goin' to a powerful lot of trouble for a few acres of land, when there's the Staked Plain only fifty miles away offerin' just as many thousands of acres as you like to put your name to.'

They stood up and gazed across the Colorado river, a mile south of Dead End, as if hoping that sight of the brown, fast-running river would give them inspiration. But none came.

Alf York sank back slowly on to the ground. Idly he picked a piece of dry grass and chewed on it. He was thinking, Bonnie watching intently. 'About your idea, Bonnie.'

'Yes?' — eagerly.

'It might work at that.'

She heard Frank M'Cone sigh, as if he had wanted to hear the big storekeeper reach that opinion. The two men smoked in silence for a minute, and then Alf spoke again.

'It kinda puts a different complexion on things, that idea o' your'n, Bonnie. I reckon it could make the Laramies a bit cautious ef they found themselves gettin' hurt every time they went out an' hurt somebody else.'

'An eye fer an eye,' nodded Frank M'Cone approvingly.

'You think you'll get support for — for these night riders?' asked Bonnie breathlessly. She was looking ahead. Once they got some movement directed against the crooked element of Dead End and she felt certain that inevitably it would grow, and the logical end to such growth of public feeling would be the establishment of real justice and order in the county. Then her fine old grandfather's death would be avenged.

'Yeah, I reckon we c'n raise a vigilance organization. Thar's men who will take guns an' ride pervided they don't have to do it in daytime — them Laramies shore can be powerful bitter agen people they think is agen 'em.'

'Shore,' came Frank M'Cone's voice. 'I reckon we c'n raise twenty hard-ridin' quick-shooting young fellars who'll be real glad ter smack back at the almighty Laramies. This night ridin' idea shore will tickle 'em.'

Alf interposed drily, 'It shore will, but you got to remember one thing, Frank. Night ridin' agen the Laramies puts us agen the law.'

'The law?' exclaimed Bonnie. 'Why, it's to establish law and order that it will be done!'

'The law,' reminded Alf heavily, 'is represented by Sher'f Jed Louen hereabouts, don't forgit. It'll give the Laramies excuse ter string up any night rider they catch a holt on.'

'Yes,' whispered Bonnie, her lovely face looking troubled, 'I hadn't thought of that. It makes the mission dangerous — they'll carry their lives in their hands.'

'We'll get the men ter do it, all the same,' said M'Cone abruptly, rising. 'I'll go round the ranches near by my place an' find out who'll ride. Reckon we'd better meet at your place in three days' time an' let you know the result, Alf.'

So it was arranged. Alf would send a man to carry the word round to the people he trusted all east of Dead End. Frank M'Cone would recruit west of the town, where he lived. They would meet in three days' time and see if they'd raised enough night riders to be able to take on the formidable Laramie organization.

They rose to go. Alf warned Bonnie not to return home in case Jed Louen had left men there to wait for her, so she decided to wait until dark and then ride up to George and Alice Wheatcroft's place, close by the old Bull Ford. They'd take care of her.

They went back to their horses, the two men to ride away. Bonnie helped Frank M'Cone hoist up his sacks of supplies. He said he could do without his water-bottle, and he also left her a can of beans and another of tomatoes. That would keep the hunger away until she was able to ride off to the Wheatcrofts'.

Big, fat Alf York was actually in the saddle when he began to talk about the bounty man. Bonnie found herself going rigid, her head bent as she listened intently.

'Shows you never c'n tell,' came Alf's voice down to her. 'That bounty man, now — wal. I reckon no one hereabouts has ever bin heard to say a good word about a bounty man. I'd have said they was worse than the varmints they took up.' He sighed and shifted in the unaccustomed saddle.

'An' that's whar we was all wrong. That bounty man was straight — an' clean. Some people back in Dead End knew of him an' talked when he had gone. He was just a quiet fellar mindin' his own business when he saw a sight that sickened him.

'A couple ornery cayuses lay fer a storekeeper — a tenderfoot who had come to set up in Stampede, an' had brought his wife an' baby with him. Green he was, but he had guts. These cayuses walked in on him and demanded the money in his drawer. Wal, I reckon that fellar needed all the money he'd got, what with a wife an' child, so he stood in their way and wouldn't give it to 'em.'

'And they shot him?' That was Bonnie's voice. All too well she had heard similar tales before.

'Yeah, they shot him. Both of 'em. Shot him with his wife lookin' on. Then

164

they walked across his body, helped themselves to everything they fancied, and rode on to the nearest saloon to spend their ill-gotten gains.'

'And no one touched them?'

'A lotta people wanted to, but these fellars was bad — real pisen. They swaggered round that town darin' people to shoot at 'em.'

'Knowin' no one would shoot them from behind like the rats they are,' broke in Bonnie impetuously. 'Oh, I know all about the Texas code of honour. They don't dare shoot it out face to face because they know they haven't a chance in a straight draw against professional gunmen, and they won't shoot 'em from behind in case someone calls them cowards after-wards. That's why these low-down killers get away with their crimes so often.'

Frank M'Cone spat expressively.

'She's right, Alf. That's how it is — often, I reckon.'

'But the bounty hunter,' broke in

Bonne eagerly. 'What did he do?'

'He came ridin' into town after the shootin'. He heard the woman cryin', an' he went in an' saw her sittin' beside her poor husband's body. So he went into town to shoot it out with the killers, only they'd just rode out a little while before.

'It made him good an' mad that they'd got away with it. They say he was normally a quiet sort of fellar, but he sure cussed 'em good and proper fer lettin' the varmints get away. Someone called out that he'd taken care to ride in after they'd left, so at that he stands up and says, 'Fix a bounty on them snakes' heads, an' I'll go trail 'em to the Yukon ef necessary an' bring 'em back fer a rope necktie.'

'That didn't get 'em subscribin' ter any bounty until he said he wouldn't take the bounty ef he won it — there was that poor widder an' kid could do with it ter keep the store goin'.'

'So that's why he turned bounty man!' Bonnie's eyes were shining. 'Oh,

Mr York, I always felt that Tom M'Grea was no low-down bounty hunter. Why — why, it was wonderful, doing a thing like that!'

She turned from her horse so that they couldn't see her face. She didn't know why, but with the gladness of knowing had come a warm flush to her cheeks. She didn't want them to notice it, neither did she want them to see the sparkle in her eyes.

'And to think I nearly let his prisoners go — I nearly cheated him out of the success he'd won!'

Then the lights went out of her eyes; swiftly she turned her face up to Alf York's, and now it was mournful. 'Oh, Mr York, I was so bitter to him before I left. I said things to hurt him!'

'It won't stop him from gettin' through with his prisoners, I reckon,' said Alf York drily.

'No,' whispered Bonnie, 'but he'll never forgive me for it.' And now it seemed vitally necessary to her happiness that he should forgive her.

Then they rode away, leaving a girl filled with bittersweet emotions — sweet because she had never wanted to feel that big Tom M'Grea was just another callous, conscienceless bounty hunter — bitter because the things she had said seemed likely to impair any prospects of a future friendship between them.

After the two horsemen had disappeared she went back into the drowsy shade and slept until it was coming dark. Then she opened the cans, ate most of the contents, drank what was left in the water-bottle and prepared to ride off to the Wheatcrofts'.

She rode carefully, keeping to the soft ground at the side of the trail. She had all the time in the world, and she wasn't going to fall into the hands of any of the Laramie faction if she could help it.

So it was that when she heard horsemen riding along the trail towards Dead End she was able to pull into the safety of a shadowy rock-outcrop and remain there unseen while they passed.

They were the only people she met, and they proved no trouble to her.

Yet all the rest of the way to the Wheatcrofts' her mind was a frantic jumble of fears and speculations.

For as he passed one of the riders had sworn at his tired horse, had urged it into better pace.

And Bonnie felt as near certain as anyone can be that that voice from the dark was — Dutch George's.

8

The Coming of the Red Men

They were thrilling days that followed for Bonnie, hiding out at the Wheatcrofts'. At last it seemed as though the tide was turning; at last they seemed to have fallen on an idea that permitted cautious men to strike back at the arrogant, powerful Laramie organization, with their tough, trigger-quick cowboys and bodyguard of imported professional killers.

George Wheatcroft made a point of riding over each day to see Alf York and find out progress. York's nephew, a hard-riding man of twenty, was making the rounds. Each night he circled back into Dead End to report to his uncle, only to take the trail again with first light next morning. It was a big country, and sometimes he called on no more than three or four places in a day.

But he'd got two good men to join the night riders on his first day — two of the men he had gone to see. Maybe he could have got more, but he knew these boys and trusted them, and he didn't dare disclose their plans to anyone less trustworthy, so he kept his mouth shut except when he was with friends.

Even so he had five turn-downs that day. Three were pretty reasonable — they were in the midst of cutting out some diseased cattle that threatened the herd. But the other two . . .

'Cold feet,' he said contemptuously to his uncle. 'They said all sorts of things, but I reckon it added up ter that in the end.'

'Are they safe?' Fat old Alf York looked quickly up across the table.

'They won't talk,' said the boy ominously, stuffing himself with beef and beans. 'I told 'em ef they talked they'd get strung up by the night riders. Guess they're as scared of us as the

Laramies now,' he ended with a grin. He was a good, resourceful cow-puncher, just the kind they needed.

Next day he rode in to say he'd got five good men and one turn-down only, but his last day wasn't so good because the men he had trailed twenty miles to see were off hunting wild horses. He got one volunteer only.

Alf looked at Coogan.

'That's the way it always is,' said the corn-chandler, bitterly. 'Nothin' ever goes right, not even the best of ideas. We've got less than a dozen men after three days' work.'

Alf was more of a philosopher.

'That leaves only about eight needed from up-river. We won't start gettin' sore until we hear from Frank M'Cone. Guess he'll be in mighty soon now.'

Someone else came in before M'Cone, however — Bonnie.

The door of the York kitchen opened suddenly and Bonnie's smiling face popped in. Mrs York's spectacles dropped from her nose in astonishment, while big, heavy Alf lumbered to his feet in something almost approaching anger.

'Bonnie, what in the tarnation are you doing in Dead End? You should have stayed hid with the Wheatcrofts —'

Bonnie calmly stripped off her gloves and shoved them into the pockets of her jeans. Defiantly she pushed back her hat.

'I wanted to be in on anything that happened tonight,' she told them. Then she seemed to melt and become appealing girlhood. 'After all, it was my idea, Mr York, and — and I felt terrible, cooped up at the Wheatcrofts. I just had to ride in.'

'Wal, I guess now you're hyar you'd better stay,' growled old Alf, but he was uneasy.

The whole idea of the night-riding vigilantes was fraught with the danger that could come from betrayal. A lot of people had heard the whisper by now, and perhaps even the seemingly trusty might go over and talk to the enemy.

They sat in that big kitchen, the lamp throwing its yellow light on them. Coogan had come in early, to be followed by limping Kurt Reimer, the settler from Germany.

When Kurt saw Bonnie he pretended to be indignant.

'She iss a hoss-thief, that gal. She shore will dekerate a tree some day, you see ef she don't!'

But then he laughed. In the fight against the lawless element of Dead End he considered the loan of one of his best horses a little price to pay.

'It iss all I c'n do,' he explained philosophically. 'I cannot fight. All right, my hosses for me will haff ter do the fightin'.'

Rube Thompson came in also. He was a bit arrogant because he was young and contemptuous of old Alf York's way of running a cowtown store, and since he and his brother started up in opposition they had done pretty well. All the same he was sound, and old Alf rather liked the pair. Joe, Rube's brother, couldn't get round because he had to weigh up a lot of groceries that had come in by ox freighter that afternoon.

They didn't talk much, sitting in the lamplight. They were waiting for Frank M'Cone's report and weren't interested in conversation outside it.

Bonnie sat among them, trembling with excitement. It seemed certain now that her plan would come about. It was impossible to think that Frank M'Cone wouldn't have raised at least half a dozen trustworthy supporters from his bend of the river — more likely he'd have approached and won over at least a dozen.

A dozen — two dozen night riders in all — not a lot to face a vicious mob of around sixty from the big Laramie holdings, but with the element of surprise always in their favour they could create havoc with their swift night raids.

Even, thought Bonnie, with a few less they could still ride out and make successful sorties against their powerful adversaries, and she began to think of the things that could be done to rattle and weaken the enemy.

There was so much a resolute band could do against the Laramies — but it had to be a pretty big band for such operations. As old Alf York kept insisting, they needed around twenty, and that number would be all too small if at any time they were surprised by the Laramies' superior forces.

About ten o'clock Alf York became uneasy.

'I figgered Frank wouldn't be late,' he said, 'but maybe he don't intend ter come tonight.'

'Or mebbe something's happened to him,' broke in old Coogan, then his eyes flickered towards Bonnie as if regretting his natural pessimism.

Bonnie thought: 'Yes, anything could have happened to him.' And then everybody began to get uneasy at Coogan's words, began to think what it could mean to them.

Rube Thomson suddenly stood up. He was no coward, but he was no fool, either.

'Mebbe it's not a good thing that we're all sittin' in hyar,' he told them abruptly. 'Ef someone's talked outa turn an' Frank M'Cone's bin took up by the new sher'f, then mebbe we c'n expect a visit from the Laramie mob.'

Alf hoisted himself out of his chair.

'Reckon you're right, Rube.'

He took down an old rifle that he hadn't used since the days six years before when he'd come crawling into Dead End with his store packed into a dilapidated prairie schooner. Then he'd had to fight a few times to keep good his claim to the supplies he had brought.

He slipped some shells into the magazine, then crossed to a window that gave a view down the shadowy alley. If trouble opened up when his friends started to leave, Alf reckoned to be on hand to cover them with his trusty rifle.

Rube said:

'I'll go first.'

He was no coward, and, he was willing to be first to run into trouble if it was waiting for them out in the alley.

It was.

Lead screeched into the woodwork of the door not two inches from his left ear, gouging out splinters that ripped blood in a line of fine beads from his neck. Someone laughed simultaneously with the shot — the sort of laugh you might expect from a guy with crazy blue eyes.

Old Alf let fly as Rube crashed frantically back into the room, seeking cover. Coogan kicked the door to and grabbed his first model Colt — nearly as old as himself, people used to say.

Alf didn't hit anything, but it must have been near, because it stopped short the laughter which changed to a quick curse. Then there was silence, a silence broken only by a distant drumming of horses' hoofs coming into town.

Alf peered cautiously down the alley. At the end, the only way out, the light from Milligan's saloon feebly lit up the buildings that stood on either side of the alley. There were long dark shadows there among the warm yellow patches of light from the saloon. His eyes getting used to the light, Alf decided there were three shadows down the alley that must originate from men in the street outside.

Then he saw a movement and wondered if there were four men down there. The voice stopped cursing. Silence for a second, save for the rapid advance of those flying hoofs. Then Jed Louen's voice:

'We know the gal's thar with you, York — that Bonnie Hayday that's wanted fer helpin' a criminal ter get away. Send her down alone an' we won't do no harm to you, mebbe.'

Alf pulled trigger and shouted: 'Mebbe!' at the same instant. The bullet gouged a hole through the end of the building from which the voice had come.

Kurt Reimer called:

'That building iss mine, Alf York! Do not too many bullets in it put!'

Bonnie came across to fighting old Alf, his fat cheeks falling in folds over the stock of his rifle. She had the impression that the old storekeeper was getting quite a kick out of the unexpected battle.

'Oh dear, it looks as though I was seen coming into town! I'm sorry — I brought trouble on you.'

Alf cuddled his rifle and didn't take his eyes off the alley end.

'Better that way than ter find, as we suspected, that Frank M'Cone's bin caught out. Now, that would ha' bin bad, 'cause then the whole idea of the night riders would be busted.'

Bonnie said wretchedly:

'All the same, I'm — I'm sorry. This is going to mean awful trouble to you. Stop firing.'

Alf lifted one eye to her.

'Whar you think you're goin'?'

'To give myself up.' She pulled on her gloves. 'I can't bring more trouble on you.'

Alf laughed as if the thought of trouble wasn't unpleasant.

'You' ain't goin' out,' he told her. 'Not until we take you out ourselves. Hell, gal, you don't think we'd let you fall into the hands of a pisenous reptile like Loco Lou, now do you?'

Old Coogan, flourishing his ancient Colt, advised:

'You stay put, honey. Mebbe things'll just work out. They gener'ly do, I reckon.'

Which was unusually optimistic, coming from an old pessimist like Coogan.

But when Bonnie turned she saw the concern and worry on Mrs York's face, and it confirmed her own fears. Things were going to be unpleasant for her friends if she stayed. Jed Louen was the law, and he had plenty of supporters.

Alf jerked his head erect, listening.

'Goldarn it,' he swore. 'Don't them fellars know they're in town?'

For the flying hoofs were right in among the buildings now, and their pace was still unslackened. Listening, Bonnie had an impression of horses being flogged even on the last stages of their journey.

The shooting must have brought men to the doors of Milligan's, and now they could be heard pouring into the street, maybe also to see what the horsemen were up to. A roar of excited voices went up, as if the riders had been recognized. It was tantalizing, back in Alf's store, to hear the hubbub and not know what it was all about.

Then a horseman crashed into view right at the end of the alley. The quick eyes of the storekeeper recognized the rider as he flung himself off his mount.

'Frank!' he exclaimed. 'Frank M'Cone's rid through at last!'

But the way he had come was disturbing. Clearly there was something wrong to bring him riding into town in this wild manner — and by the sound of it he had not ridden in alone.

Along the main street they could hear men shouting, and now came the sound of horses whinnying with fright, the sound as their hoofs lashed out and made contact with board walls. And over all the high sustained note of men shouting in crazy excitement.

Frank came off his horse at the run and let it career away into the dark. He almost fell into the alley, then recovered and came staggering to his feet.

Alf's finger took first pressure on his rifle trigger as he saw the threatening movement of those shadows at the end of the alley.

Then Louen's voice. 'Whar you goin', stranger? What'n hell's all the shoutin' about?'

Frank went back quietly against the alley wall at sound of that dangerous voice. He was panting for breath, but caution showed in his voice when he spoke. He wasn't giving Loco Lou a chance to use those deadly guns if he could help it.

'Thar's bin a massacre,' he shouted, and in the store they knew he was lifting his voice so that they, too, could hear. That was just in case anything happened to him.

'Thar's a million red devils pourin' out of the Staked Plains. They're burnin' up the countryside, drivin' off the cattle, an' scalpin' every man, woman, an' child they can lay thar tomahawks into.'

'A million?' said Louen.

'That's how it looked.' M'Cone was so out of breath he could hardly speak. 'I've never seen so many Injuns in all my born days. Thar's thousands, I'd say, layin' waste up river. The Henneker ranch has gone. So has Culbertson's. My place was burnin' when I rode out. Back along the Court Valley thar's a battle goin' on. Court an' his men are surrounded in their rancho. Good job it's 'dobe, or they'd never be able to hold off the varmints. I met the Lee brothers ridin' in fer help. Their family's all gone, too. We're raisin' all the men we can ter go back an' help Court get out.'

As the recital of disaster unfolded the listeners in Alf York's kitchen looked at each other in concern and horror. This was a major Indian uprising by the sound of it. Not for years had there been so much damage done by an Indian raid.

Coogan blinked at Alf. 'Now we got Injuns ter fight, as well as the Laramies.'

Alf nodded, squinting down his barrel. 'Shore. This puts an end ter vigilantes an' night ridin' agen the Laramie bunch. Reckon it'll be every man needed fer a drive agen the Comanches.'

'Yeah — the Comanches.' Coogan nodded. He didn't need to be pessimistic now; the Comanches would supply all that for him.

Then Louen was speaking, shouting because of the truly frantic noise in the street back of him. 'I'm goin' back to see how things are. You wait hyar an' get Bonnie Hayday. She's not gettin' away from me. Plug her ef she tries ter make a break fer it.'

9

Blackmask

Frank M'Cone started to edge up the alley. Louen's voice rang out. 'You hold your boots, mister. One more stride an' the toes'll turn up — permanent.'

Frank M'Cone froze against the wall. They could see him as a silhouette against the yellow lights from Milligan's deserted saloon. They heard the sound of Sheriff Jed Louen's high heels as he drummed along the board sidewalk, but it quickly became lost in the noise down the street.

Bonnie licked her lips. 'Now what do we do?'

'You don't move outa this door, Bonnie. Reckon them merchants might pull trigger outa nervousness at seein' you. Stay right whar you are.'

Men were riding out of town now as

they found their horses, and the hubbub was noticeably dying with the decrease in numbers out on the main street. Inside the kitchen they stood and waited in silence. An old clock ticked away the seconds with a noise like a rusty old woodpecker.

Then Alf and Coogan, sharing the one alley window now, became rigid, watching.

For Frank was coming slowly away from the wall, his hands lowering. They waited for a shot to end his life, but it didn't come. They even felt that Frank was surprised by it all.

Then Frank came hurrying up the alley. Half-way along he called: 'Bonnie, come out quickly. Now's your chance ter git away!'

Alf's big hand dropped on her shoulder, restraining her.

'This is somethin' I don't understand,' he growled uneasily. 'Them fellars is still thar, 'cause I c'n see their shadows. Maybe they're makin' a trap fer you through M'Cone.' His eyes narrowed so much they were nearly lost in the folds of fat above his cheeks.

Coogan said unhappily: 'I didn't think M'Cone was a fellar like that. I reckoned he'd be the kind ter die rather than git a gal in trouble with scum like that.'

Then Frank's frantic voice: 'C'mon — c'mon, Bonnie! Thar's a gun stickin' in these critters' backs!'

That settled it. They didn't know who was holding the guns, but it explained the mystery of this chance to escape.

Alf brought his rifle down and lurched to the door. 'Take your chance, Bonnie. Lit out fer your hoss. I'll contact you at the Wheatcrofts when I want you.'

Bonnie started running. She ran into the alley, her feet beating a rapid, echoing tattoo. Frank grabbed her by the hand and hustled her to the rail under Kurt Reimer's overhanging building. She mounted and pulled her horse round.

As she straightened in the saddle she saw two shadows at the mouth of the alley.

And back of them was a third dark shadow.

As she jumped her horse into its stride she bent forward, shouting: 'Thanks, mister. Thanks a lot.'

And then she went cold, for the head turned and she found herself looking into a menacing, black-masked face.

She found, herself riding through a confusion of men and horses. Every door was open along that street; every building poured light into the night's blackness. And men were racing from building to building, collecting ammunition, borrowing water-bottles, new harness — everything required for them to campaign against the warring Redskins.

As fast as they were equipped they sought out their horses and went thundering off into the dark. Bonnie, hat down to prevent recognition, thought: That's funny. You couldn't get 'em to stand up to the Laramie mob, even when they were being hustled around and shot at. But the moment a Redskin shows up they forget their wives and sweethearts, their cattle and ranches, and go off to drive 'em back.

But it wasn't past understanding. The red man was the first enemy, and so often had these Westerners been called to defend themselves against the Indians that it was instinctive now, this action of banding themselves together the moment danger threatened from the Redksins. The Laramie danger was different. The enemy was in their midst and powerful. They had had little experience of fighting their own kind, and didn't yet know how to get down to it. Silver Sam had been first to start them on the right track with his talk of sheriffs and law and order. And, curiously, Bonnie had given the second lead in demanding vigilantes.

Bonnie crouched low over the big bay and felt the mighty legs stab out like powerful pistons. They rocked out of town, into the blackness of the countryside — a blackness the more intense because of the yellow light so lately in her eyes. As she rode her bewildered mind speculated on the identity of the masked man in those deep shadows at the end of the alley.

Who could it be who had come at such a timely moment to her rescue?

And for some reason she found herself thinking of — the Easterner, the man who had the name of Hayday in that red leather pocketbook.

Five minutes along the trail and she heard a sound behind her. Someone was riding rapidly in her rear. She touched her heels into her horse's sides and increased its pace. Turning in the saddle, she listened. The pounding hoofs came on.

She thought: 'That fellar's followin' me,' and bent low over her horse again and told him to give her all he had. He did. When next she pulled up there was no sound from the rear. Whoever it was had lost the trail.

She rode up to the Wheatcrofts' wondering who her pursuer had been — the masked man or one of the Louen posse. She thought the latter. Louen wouldn't have been long in returning, most likely, and he'd start a pursuit, badly wanting her as he did.

She came tiredly into the Wheatcrofts' with her news of the onsurge of savage red men down the valley. They listened in consternation, then George Wheatcroft went to get his gun. They watched him in silence; they knew that all down the valley it would be the same — as the menfolk got the news they would reach for their guns and ride out.

Alice Wheatcroft said wearily: 'There'll be pickings for the Laramies after this. I reckon there'll be plenty of land wanting new owners after this fight's over.'

George looked up from the cartridge belt he was filling. 'Mebbe the Laramies will do their share of fightin' an' get knocked off themselves.'

Bonnie said: 'Mebbe. But I don't see

the Laramies ridin' off as you're doin'. They're the kind to let you people do the fightin' while they sit back an' scoop the pool.'

George Wheatcroft swore. 'By heck, that's somethin' people won't stand for!'

Bonnie's voice was bitter. 'They'll have to stand for it, George. After this fightin' the Laramies will be stronger than ever.'

It was a sound prophecy. Within days they were to see how right the girl was. With all the menfolk gone except for a couple of *peon* hands, Alice and Bonnie had to take their turn with the work. Bonnie browned her hands and face and stuck on a sombrero, and they reckoned she would pass for a Mexican boy at almost any distance. Then she went out on the everlasting work of blocking broken fences, driving in strays from the scrub where the senseless beasts would die of thirst if they weren't brought to water, cutting out sickly beasts who might infect the whole herd, and a thousand other jobs that makes up the life of a cowboy.

It was hard work, but all her adult life she had shared in it, and now she stuck it better than Alice Wheatcroft, the ex-school marm.

News came drifting down the valley to them, sometimes through talk picked up by the Mexicans, but once when Alice Wheatcroft rode into town for supplies.

Alf York, Coogan, Rube Thomson, Kurt Reimer and Frank M'Cone were in gaol. Jed Louen had been furious at the way he had been outwitted, and when he found the girl gone he had clapped her friends behind bars in an instant. Bonnie breathed a sigh of relief at the news. She had dreaded far worse information. At least her friends were alive, and perhaps they wouldn't be in gaol for long.

The next news was that the Laramie mob down to a man were around town or out at the Circle ranch. As Bonnie had cynically prophesied, they were leaving the fighting to others — they weren't risking their hides.

But the news they were waiting for, because it was even more vital to all of them on the Rio Colorado, took time to get around to them.

Some wounded straggled back into Dead End. They told of vicious, bitter fighting. Already over twenty settlers up the valley were known to be dead, and nobody could guess at the number of wounded.

The Court rancho was still holding out, though all the barns and outbuildings had gone up in flames and the cattle had been driven into the hills. The wounded told of a massing of men among the pine bluffs over the hill from Court Valley. Reinforcements were pouring in from all over the countryside. When the white men decided they were strong enough to attack, this was going to assume the proportions of a battle.

The attack must have come later that day, and news of victory for the settlers was brought in by an excited boy who had been sent back to order a wagonload of ammuntion and food to be rushed out.

It was a victory, but it had been bought dearly. There were many dead, said the boy. And he was a typical frontier kid. He opined wisely: 'Guess that's not the last we've heard of them Comanches. Reckon they'll rest up a while then have another lick at us.'

And that was the opinion of the men who came down later from the foothills where the fighting had taken place.

The Indians were massing all up the valleys. They had been defeated in the first big encounter, and had suffered considerable losses. Nevertheless, they were in such numbers that they were able to stand such losses — perhaps, in fact, the reinforcements that were pouring over the hills more than made up for their losses.

'At any time now I guess them blamed Redskins'll come a-rampagin' out agen,' a rancher told the people bluntly. 'We might lick 'em agen, but ef we do we'll be in no condition ter stand another battle. In the end they're bound to break through, and then there'll be no stopping 'em this side of the river. They'll burn out this blamed town an' loot every ranch fer twenty miles down river within a day,' he shouted.

It stirred the crowd to hear such a threatening situation outlined for them. They were mostly old men, with a few boys and a handful of women. But among them stood the smiling, cynical Jed Louen and his recently recruited deputy sheriffs, Mick Wade with a bandage round his gun-hand, Alec Fergie, Montana Regan, Maxill, Coltas and two or three of the gambling men.

Someone shouted: 'How 'bout getting the Army in on this, Pete?'

The rancher shrugged his dusty shoulders contemptuously. 'What army? Twenty stuffed soldiers down at San Antonio with a gun as old as themselves. Mebbe a hundred up at Fort

Worth who'll take a week ter git the girths on the fat bellies of their grass-fed hosses. No, this is a fight we've got to win ourselves — nobody else c'n win it for us.'

He drew a deep breath. The rancher had been one of Silver Sam's supporters. 'Every man who can bear arms must go up ter meet the Injuns when next they attack. Ef we c'n defeat 'em decisively next time, mebbe they won't come a third time. But we've got ter have every man-jack up thar that c'n fight.'

He was looking angrily towards the professional gunmen and gamblers. They gave back look for look. Jed Louen even laughed. He wasn't a man to feel ashamed.

The rancher lost his head a little. 'What'n the tarnation are you fellars goin' ter do about it?' he shouted, and his accusing finger pointed from one puncher to another. 'Thar's not a man from the Laramie outfit who's up thar fightin' — not one, I tell you. An' the

Laramie outfit is the biggest round here.'

The people didn't need to be told that. They knew that the Laramies had almost as many men in their employ as there were lying up in the mesquite at that moment waiting for the expected Indian attack.

The old men stirred and muttered, but the women were bolder, and shouted: 'Shame! They oughta be hung, lettin' our men do the fightin' for 'em!'

The rancher quietened the crowd with a lift of his hand. Deliberately he addressed Louen.

'You're sher'f hyar. Why ain't you up thar takin' charge o' the fightin? Why ain't them blamed dep'ties o' your'n ridin' up to help our men?'

Louen laughed. Laughed and showed his contempt for all of them. He sauntered forward easily, his face derisive.

'Reckon I'm keepin' my men back just in case them Injuns does break through. Mebbe then you old men an'

women'll be glad ter have some fightin'
men to protect you, huh?'

But they weren't to be deceived. They
knew that Jed Louen and his gunnies
were staying back from the fighting
because cynically they thought it smart
to let others do the fighting for them.
And if the Indians did break through to
Dead End, Louen and his men weren't
likely to stay and do any fighting in an
effort to protect the women and
children. Their kind took to their horses
at such moments.

Sheriff Louen was standing there,
jeering at them all, arrogant in his
strength. Then an old man on the fringe
of the crowd lifted his voice and
quavered: 'Look out, thar! There's the
bounty man agen!'

Louen came whipping round, his
mouth a vicious snarl. Like magic there
were six-guns in his hands.

And then the crowd started to laugh
at him, to jeer at him in turn. For there
was no bounty man, it was a trick of
that cunning old-timer to upset the

cocky sheriff. And it had upset him.

'Smart, huh?' he snarled, ramming his guns back into their holsters. 'But some day I'm gonna meet up with that bounty man, and when I do — '

His voice trailed off and his audience were silent. This sheriff of theirs was crazy, and the things a crazy man could do to a man who had humbled him weren't lightly to be contemplated.

Alice Wheatcroft rode back with the story. She also told Bonnie that the deputation had ridden across to the Laramie ranch to appeal for aid.

'But they won't get it,' said Bonnie cynically.

'You don't think so?'

'I know.' Bonnie walked restlessly across to the window. 'And why? Pedro came in with the news today. Burt Laramie's had every man on a big drive bringing all his cattle down from the north and fording them across the river. They're working night and day, and he's got lamps fixed up to guide the night herders. They say he's stringin' barbed wire on the south bank, and he's got a boatful of dynamite to turn loose if a mob of Indians tries to rush the ford.'

Alice spoke bitterly. 'He's lucky, having a south bank to hide out on. We people on the north bank must stay an' fight it out. What's more, we're having to fight it out for Burt Laramie and his brothers.'

It made her boil to think of that powerful Laramie outfit being concerned only with saving their cattle at this moment and doing nothing about the common safety.

Bonnie said, half-turning to look out of the window: 'You don't know everything, though. You know Jesse Hamble got killed when they went out to attack the Indians?' Hamble was a smallholder like Frank M'Cone, with about two hundred head of Herefords which he was hoping to build into a fine herd.

Alice nodded expectantly.

'The Laramies have picked up the

Herefords in their drive and taken them across the river. Pedro says he thinks they are brand blotting over the other side.'

The ex-school marm exclaimed:

'That's the limit, stealing cattle from a dead man. The low-down, thievin' lot.'

But Bonnie wasn't listening. Hadn't heard a word of what her friend was saying. For she was rigid with horror.

She had turned . . . and within a foot of her a man was standing looking in at the window — the Easterner.

10

The Easterner

Bonnie stepped back, her eyes widening with horror at being discovered in her hideout. Mentally she blamed herself for not keeping a better watch on the long straight track across the mesquite. Then she remembered her disguise, and turned quickly in the forlorn hope that the Easterner wouldn't have recognized her.

The door was open because of the heat. Three strides from the window and the stranger was looking in at them through the doorway. He was polite, removing his hat to Alice Wheatcroft.

'I sure apologize fer intrudin' on you. Didn't think there was anyone here as I rode in, though.'

Alice, flustered, said:

'That's all right. Come in and make

yourself at home, stranger.' She shot an urgent glance at Bonnie, who was backing out of the room. The stranger was standing watching her.

'All right, Pedro, you can go,' said Alice to cover Bonnie's retreat, and the girl ducked her head as a house-boy would do and dodged back into the kitchen. Inside, though, she halted with her back to the door, listening.

'That Mex shore had got blue eyes,' came the thin Yankee voice of their visitor.

'I've seen many a Mex with blue eyes,' retorted Alice Wheatcroft. 'Plenty.'

'Plenty? Now, I wouldn't say plenty. A few, maybe.' He paused, then said, 'You don't see many Mexican house-boys wearin' their sombreros around the house, either.'

'He'd just come in from drivin' cattle.'

'A houseboy drive cattle?' They knew by the way he persisted on the subject that he was suspicious. 'Most house-boys I know jes' don't know one end of a cow from the other.'

'Everyone's got to help, with the men away,' Alice retorted.

'The men are all away? All of 'em?'

Alice hesitated. It wasn't, maybe, a good thing to tell a strange Yankee there were only women around the place. But then she'd already let the information slip out, so she nodded. Even so, she didn't cotton on to this stranger whose every sentence was a question.

'That's too bad.' The stranger sighed and rose to his feet, though he'd just sat down. From his tweed-jacket inside pocket he took out a red-leather notebook. Peeping through a crack in the rough plank door, Bonnie recognized it.

He read out from it:

'George MacDonald Wheatcroft. That your husband's name?'

'It is.' Alice looked at that red notebook in astonishment. She couldn't understand why a Yankee should have written her husband's name in a book, and she felt that the solution could hardly be reassuring. Bonnie, listening, could understand how she felt because that was the way she had been when the Yankee read the name of Hayday from that mysterious pocketbook.

'Why?' Alice blurted as the Easterner started to tuck the book away.

'That's a subject I c'n only discuss with your husband, and that only ef he's got the deeds of ownership of this land.'

'Deeds?' Vaguely Alice felt that here was the menace she had suspected. 'We bought this land at San Antonio office. It cost five dollars an acre, and we got the Government grant of two dollars an acre when we bought. We've got all the papers, and no one's going to say we're not entitled to our land.'

She was suddenly fierce, angry. Out West they were touchy over matters concerning ownership. Many a man had built up a holding, only to see someone walk on to it with some title deeds that had better approval than his own. Now, Alice Wheatcroft suspected some such trick, especially in the absence of her menfolk.

But he surprised her. His nasal voice exclaimed drily:

'Madam, I guess no one's goin' ter say that. An' fer your sake I'm real glad.'

He gave a little bow and started off for the door. Alice forgot her suspicions now and exclaimed:

'For land's sake, what's it mean, all this talk about deeds?'

The Easterner shrugged.

'You'll find out soon enough.' Then he looked at the door through which Bonnie had passed and said distinctly, 'You wouldn't know whar I could find a gal called Bonnie Hayday? A right nice gal even though thar's a hundred dollars reward out fer her.'

'No.' Bonnie's best friend spoke abruptly, fiercely.

'A pity,' sighed the Yankee. 'I want ter see that gal.' Then he said, abruptly, 'Guess thar's others lookin' fer her right now also.'

'Meanin'?'

'That loco sher'f from Dead End is searching every building down the valley in the hope of findin' her. They tell me she knows whar the bounty man is, an' Jed Louen opins ter carve out the guts o' that critter on his Bowie knife. Some day I'm goin' ter find out what the bounty man did ter Louen ter make him so sore.'

Alice Wheatcroft heard her voice saying:

'He kicked the new sheriff into unconciousness.' But she was thinking frantically of other things. 'You say they're searching?'

'Yep. I came down ahead of 'em, but they've bin ter El Paso, Ramirez Ranchov, an' all the nesters down the ford trail. I guess they'll arrive hyar within the hour. Maybe you might like ter be absent when they come, because I don't think them critters is the kind ter entertain when your menfolk are away fightin'.'

Alice's eyes widened. Suddenly she

understood that this Yankee stranger was trying to help them — tip them off, as her husband would say.

'Thanks. Thanks for telling us,' she exclaimed.

'Us?' His voice was ironic. He was looking at that kitchen door, and Alice knew then he hadn't been deceived by Bonnie's stained brown skin and tall Mexican hat.

'Yes, us.' She shrugged. It didn't matter what she said now. 'Next time you come I'll be politer to you, stranger.'

'Next time I come I'll maybe tell you things that'll rejoice your heart,' he said. He had a thin, whining, unpleasant voice, but she was realizing that that didn't mean a thing. He meant well for them and there was humour in him.

He went out and caught his horse. When he was mounted he looked up the broad valley.

'Looks like you're goin' ter have visitors quicker'n I thought,' he said cheerfully, and then spurred off.

Away across the old border trail she could see a distant cloud of dust that told of several riders approaching in a hurry. She shouted to Bonnie, but the girl had heard everything and was already in the stables behind getting out their horses.

Alice scrambled up, though she was in skirts.

'Where shall we go?' she demanded.

Bonnie said, humorously:

'You c'n go where you like, Alice — I won't be with you. They're after me, and you mustn't be with me in case they catch up with us. You circle round 'em an' ride back into Dead End for more news.'

'You won't be coming back?' Alice's horse was rearing because it thought it had done enough running around for one day. She fought it down.

'Not unless I'm sure there's nobody watching the place. I'm going to sneak back to my ranch and see what's happening there.'

'Be careful,' warned Alice. 'They

were watching the place a couple of days ago.'

'They'll be tired of watching by now,' said Bonnie confidently. 'But I'll be careful — you bet I'll be careful.'

They went out of the yard with a clatter of hoofs upon stone. Just beyond the big gate they forked away from each other, Bonnie dipping quickly out of sight over the brow, Alice Wheatcroft taking the north trail that would bring her round eventually into Dead End.

As Bonnie rode she thought about the Easterner and tried to fit him into the puzzle. She wondered again if it were he who had rescued her from Louen's gunnies. Was he the masked man? If so, then it seemed that twice he had saved her. Why? What was his interest in her?

And then back she came to the red notebook.

Why was the name of Hayday in it? And now the Wheatcrofts?

It was three miles or just over to the Hayday ranch, a pleasant, wooded valley with plenty of water all the year round. She put the gallant bay to the steep slopes that guarded the ranch, then came out into the exhilarating wind on top, overlooking her home.

She sat up there on the hillside for over an hour, and in that time there was not a movement from the ranch buildings. The place had the stillness of utter desertion.

In the end worry drove caution from her mind, and she mounted and went loping down the hillside until she joined the home trail. The Hayday ranch had a foreman and two cowboys, as well as the usual Mexican house servants. The cowboys would be away with the Indian fighters, but the foreman, Ross Ankers, was an older man and would more reasonably be expected to have remained to keep the ranch going.

She was perturbed, riding slowly up the grass slope towards the white gate of the big, Spanish-style courtyard. Surely Ross and the houseboys would be around somewhere?

She dismounted and led her horse through the gateway. She called 'Ross!' approaching the wide steps that led to the shady veranda. But there was no answer. She called again, beginning to mount those steps.

And then she stopped.

For suddenly, as sure as anything she'd ever been certain in her life about before, she knew she wasn't alone just then.

She turned.

There was a cowboy standing by the white gate, a tough, leather-faced rope-slinger whom she recognized as one of the Circle boys.

Then a scraping sound brought her round again, to look up the steps towards the veranda. A cowboy was standing there, too, twin Colts drawn and raised to cover her. He had just stepped out of the house.

The cowboy with the guns grated, 'We shore had ter wait a long time fer you to come home, Bonnie Hayday.'

Evidently he had seen through her disguise.

Bonnie exclaimed quickly, 'What do you want with me? Where's my foreman and the houseboys?'

He shrugged casually. 'They're all right. They're locked up in a barn down on that bottom meadow. Guess they'll hate the smell of hay for all time now.'

He was walking down the steps, his spurs clinking with every stride. The other rope-slinger was moving with awkward bow legs to join them. The cowboy with the guns out called, 'She shore is a mighty fine piece. Mebbe we shouldn't be in a hurry to take her in ter Loco Lou. Mebbe the gal would prefer ter stop around hyar a bit with us, huh?'

She turned, her back defensively braced against the bottom post of the veranda steps. The two cowboys were coming stiffly, awkwardly, towards her, eyes gleaming, cheeks maybe a little flushed as they looked on her young beauty. There was no mercy in those faces —

Bonnie caught a movement out of her eye-corner. Looked — and saw a man's head rearing round by where the veranda turned along the south wall of the house.

She saw the black mask over the lower half of his face, just as his guns tuliped into savage, spitting flame.

The cowboy with the Colts felt them spin away — heard the blast catch up with the flying lead, then felt the awful bruising pain that followed the abrupt tearing from his grip of those heavy guns. He jumped back, clutching his numbed fingers under his arms and cursing quickly.

The masked man called, 'Shut up!' And then Bonnie knew him.

The cowboys turned, their hands grabbing for the blue Texas sky. The masked man said, 'You don't need hosses. Start walkin'. You'll mebbe reach the Circle ranch by midnight.'

The cowboys looked aghast at the

thought of being made to walk. The leather-faced rope-slinger exclaimed, 'The hell, you can't do that to a fellar, mister!'

'No? We'll see.' Another shot rang out. It kicked dust close to their feet and sent them jumping back. 'Try walkin' — or getting shot, *hombres*!'

They got it then, realized he wasn't joking. They went through the gate and started the long walk over the distant horizon, and with every stride they cursed, and while some of the curses included their boss who had planted them on the Hayday farm, most were directed against this monster with the black mask who made a fellar walk in the Texas heat.

The masked man watched them go, sheathed his guns and came slowly up to where Bonnie was standing, her hand pressed to still the beating of her heart. She looked into that black-masked face while he drawled, 'Reckon I don't want 'em to get back to their boss too soon. That wouldn't be good tactics.'

He looked at her. Bonnie said, 'You can take your mask off. I know your voice well enough.'

He tugged and the mask came down. The brown, fighting face of Big M'Grea was there. She tried to read what was in his mind, to see if there was any gladness in his eyes at sight of her, but he looked merely cool and unemotional and she felt disappointed.

But she smiled. She was glad to see him. 'Thanks for stepping in — twice. I didn't realize it was you who saved me that night Jed Louen was waiting for me to walk down that alley.'

'You told me once to look up a friend of your'n — Kurt Reimer, who has a livery stable full of no-good hosses. That night I called to see him, just as you said, but he wasn't thar.'

'He was with me up at Alf York's, only a few yards away.'

'I didn't know. I hung around in the dark, waitin' fer him to come back, but he didn't. Instead, after a time I began

ter realize that three men were watchin'
that alley mouth. When I realized that
one was my old kickin' chum, that
crazy-lookin' sher'f, I thought mebbe I
could do him no good again.'

'But you didn't.'

'Nope. He went off too quickly,
before I could work round an' get my
guns into his back. But I stuck up his
friends, all the same.'

'And thanks for doing it.'

He said, politely, 'It was a pleasure.
Afterwards I tried to catch up with you,
but my horse wasn't fast enough.'

'Oh dear!' Bonnie bit off the cry of
annoyance. To think that unwittingly
she had dodged from the man she most
wanted to meet again. To cover her
confusion she said, 'I mean, I didn't
know. Your mask made me think it
might be someone else — ' Her voice
trailed off, then, woman-like, she
started with a string of questions
— 'Why are you wearing a mask? Why
did you want to see me? How was it
you were here?'

He laughed suddenly, and it did her good to hear it. Always until now he had been too taut and grim in her presence; to hear that pleasant, almost boyish laughter was certainly a change. She found herself smiling with him.

'Gal, do you rattle off questions!' he said admiringly. 'But to answer your questions, I wear that mask around here because I don't want it known that the bounty man is back in the district. That might warn off my quarry, I guess, and I don't want that to happen.'

A sting of disappointment seemed to prick her heart at that word 'bounty'. And then she remembered this was no ordinary bounty man, and she felt ashamed for the things she had once said to him, though just now she couldn't bring herself about to apologise.

Instead she said, 'You lost your men?'

'We ran into a party of huntin' Apaches. When they realized that my Sharps was useless Dutch an' the Rattler soon gave me the slip. They ran fer it, while I had to take on a dozen braves.' He sighed. 'It shore felt tough, bringin' 'em so far an' then losin' 'em.'

'But you're on their trail again?' She had to admire the dogged, unswerving purpose of this giant cowpuncher.

'Shore. I want them five hundred dollars badly.'

'Do you know where they are?'

'Nope. I wouldn't be around this country ef I did, I reckon. Maybe they're in Arizona by now. When I heard about the Injun attack I rode out ter help the Court family. The Injuns is holed up fer the moment, so I slipped back ter see ef I could get a lead on my men and also to see you.'

'To see me?' Bonnie's heart began to hammer painfully. 'But — why?'

'I suppose,' he said calmly, 'because I like looking at you.'

She sank down on to the first step. The Circle cowboys were trudging disconsolately up the far hillside now. She felt a bit weak, curiously. Then she heard her voice quavering, 'Well, I suppose that is a reason.'

'The best,' he said simply, and then he steered away from what was developing into an embarrassing conversation. 'I figgered there was somethin' queer about this deserted rancho, so I lay up fer a while until I saw those Circle boys hidin' up fer someone. I crept up an' got into the house without 'em knowing it, a coupla hours ago, an' listened in on what they was sayin'. It was — interesting.'

She looked quickly at him, wondering what could be interesting about a pair of roughnecks' conversation. And then she remembered something. 'Your — quarry, as you call them. Do you know where they are?'

His eyes lifted. They were hard and burning. 'Ef you know, gal, you'd better tell me quick.'

Bonnie said, 'I'll make a guess. They are back in this district because I heard Dutch George's voice one night. I'll bet they've joined up with Burt Laramie, out at the Circle ranch. They're the kind of gunslingers he likes to have on his payroll.'

She had expected him to jump on his horse and ride furiously away, and she had been prepared to try to stop him, but he surprised her by seeming to relax at the words.

'That so? Dutch George is hereabouts, huh? Then I reckon that pisenous King Rattler'll be along of him.' He nodded with satisfaction. 'That's good. They c'n wait.'

'You're not going after them?' Bonnie suddenly remembered her foreman and houseboys, imprisoned in the lower barn. She started to walk down towards it, and the big bounty man fell into step by her side.

'Nope.' He answered her question after some thought. 'They're important ter me, I guess, but right now thar's only one job of real importance — fightin' them blamed Injuns. They've got ter be licked afore we start ter go fer the bad men in our crowd.'

'Like the Laramies.' Bonnie's voice was bitter.

M'Grea sighed.

'I keep hearin' the name of Laramie, an' every time it comes out it's delivered with something like a curse. Mebbe some day someone'll get around ter namin' their brand o' pisen ter me.'

Bonnie named it right then. She told him how the Laramies had come and settled into the district, and how they had grown big because they hadn't stopped at anything — even inspiring murder — in their attempts to grow.

'And just now they're not fighting the redskin. The big Laramie outfit is saving its cows while our people do the fighting for them. They don't deserve to live, those coyotes.'

Big M'Grea's face looked hard.

'Makes me feel now I should have come back with you an' fought 'em with your vigilantes.'

'It's too late for vigilantes now,' she told him. 'From what I hear when the fighting is over against the Indians we'll

have so few men left they won't be able
to start up against the Laramies ever.
And do you know what will happen?'

This was the gall of it all, the real
bitterness.

'The more men that die just now up
there, the better pleased the Laramies
will be.'

'Why?'

'Because they'll grab the land. Land's
no good to a dead man, and widows
can be shoved around pretty easily by
the Laramie mob. We've seen that
recently.'

Big M'Grea stopped and looked at
her. Then said, very softly:

'Reckon we've got to do something
about that, Bonnie, haven't we?'

Her heart bumped again, as it often
did now when he said things to her.
'We've got to do things . . . ' She liked
to find herself coupled with him in his
thoughts.

He seemed preoccupied, deep in
thought for the rest of the way to the
barn, but just as they were about to pull

down the big bars on the wide doors she asked, 'Tom. There's an Easterner riding around this country, a Yankee in dude breeches and polished leggings. Do you know who he is, or what he's doing around here?'

M'Grea shook his head.

'Nope, Bonnie, I don't. Has he — bin unpleasant to you?'

'On the contrary. I think he deliberately saved me from being captured by some of Louen's posse.'

The big door came open. On the other side were her foreman, irascible, bad-tempered but good-hearted Ross Ankers, and two uneasy Mexican boys.

The boys knew her at once, but Ross's eyes weren't so strong these days and he must have thought her to be the Mexican boy she was dressed up to represent. He began to cuss good and heartily, then Bonnie laughed and he recognized her.

They all went back to the ranch-house and sat around to wait for some coffee, but Bonnie and Big M'Grea never got it. The bounty man suddenly pulled himself out of the comfortable, buffalo-hide chair on the cool veranda and said:

'Reckon we'd better git our hosses an' ride, Bonnie.'

She saw he was looking over the rolling mesquite, saw he was significantly adjusting the guns to a more comfortable position on his thighs. She turned. There was a cloud of dust lifting over the skyline.

'Oh dear!' she sighed. 'There's no rest for an outlaw, is there, Tom?' Her eyes twinkled. 'I forgot. Maybe you don't know. There's a price on my head, Tom — a hundred dollars. And you're a bounty hunter!'

'A hundred dollars?' They were down at their horses now. 'That's a nice, tidy li'l sum. Guess I'll turn you in to the sher'f some day when I get around to such things agen, Bonnie.'

'One time I'd have believed that of you. Tom,' she laughed. 'I did say awful things to you, didn't I? I've never said sorry, but — I didn't understand. About that poor widow and her child, I mean.'

'So you know? The bounty man's not as black as he's painted, huh?' She saw his face lift in a big grin over the top of his saddle, and she knew he bore her no malice for the thoughts she had entertained. She began to think that like most big men she had met in her lifetime, he was a good-tempered, tolerant fellow, this M'Grea.

Then she remembered Dutch George and King Rattler. Both were big men. She didn't tell him that she had been outlawed through helping him to escape that day. It was something that could wait.

They mounted and loped round the backwoods, easily evading the men who sought to catch them. When they knew they were safe they sent their horses climbing into a wooded arroyo, where there was a small bubbing stream of good water and there dismounted to rest during the heat of the day.

They were lying on their backs, grateful for the cool green shade and the refreshing water, when Bonnie asked:

'What do we do now? You can't get your men until the fighting's over, and I can't get any peace because I'm an outlaw. Where are you going — and where can I go?'

'What about your friends?' He rolled over at her words, his brow furrowed.

'I don't think I can put myself on any of my friends hereabouts again,' she told him. She felt genuinely helpless and looked to the bounty man to find a solution to her problems. 'It's obvious they know I'm hiding out down river from Dead End, and they're making an intensive search for me. It won't be safe from now on for me to hide away with any of my friends, besides which it will only bring trouble to them.'

He rolled over on his back, tilted his hat over his eyes and seemed to go to sleep, but she knew he was thinking about her problem.

About five minutes later he sat up.

'Reckon thar's only one thing for it, Bonnie. I'll have ter take you with me up to the fightin'.'

11

The Apaches

He rose and in seeming abstraction began to pace the soft, yielding turf by the edge of the stream.

'It's no good goin' on like this, Bonnie,' he told her. 'You can't go on bein' an outlaw all your life.' He stopped as a thought struck him. 'I never thought ter ask, but what'n the tarnation's made a gal like you an outlaw?'

'Helping a malefactor of a bounty man to get away from a sheriff's posse,' she smiled.

He halted in astonishment.

'Oh, like that, huh? Wal, I reckon more an' more it's up ter me ter git you out of the trouble you're in. An' I think I c'n do it.'

Suddenly he came and squatted

down beside her, and he looked very big and brown as he sat hunched over her. His eyes were intent, alight with some inward fire.

'I've got a plan, Bonnie. Ef it works we c'n mebbe solve all our problems at one go. But — mebbe it won't work.'

'Tell me about it.'

He rose and started his pacing again. He wasn't a man of words and he found difficulty in expressing himself; far rather he would have been riding away into the action he contemplated.

'It jes' ain't no good, fightin' battles fer them Laramies. Our side'll come out weak and they'll be jes' that much stronger. Okay, I reckon ter win this battle agen them Comanches without much loss.'

'But how?' She couldn't understand him.

'By gittin' them Apaches ter jine in.'

'The Apaches?'

'Shore. Ef anyone hates them Comanches, it's the Apaches who got licked by 'em in the first place. I know where they are

— only a day's ride north of us. By now I guess there'll be several hundred of 'em sittin' back an' soothin' their sores. Now, ef I could git them ter jine in the fightin' they shore would turn the scales agen them Comanches.'

Bonnie looked at him with dread in her eyes.

'Tom, you're thinking of going up to those Apaches and appealing to them for aid?'

He stopped his pacing at that and grinned round at her.

'Shore, why not?' he demanded.

'But it's — it's almost suicide, riding into an Apache camp. They hate the paleface, just as much as the Comanche.'

'Right now,' he retorted, 'I figger they don't — not quite as much. Remember, it's the Comanche who's driven them off their huntin' grounds, not us. Just now I guess their bellies'll be pretty empty, because the country up north don't carry much game. Mebbe a promise of a wagon load of corn might talk in our favour.' He was still planning, working out the angles, she could see — and she could also see that nothing was going to stop him from at least trying put his plan.

She gave in.

'If it works it will certainly save a lot of our people's lives.'

'And the stronger we come out of this fight, the more likely we are to be able to turn on the Laramies afterwards. Then I get Dutch George an' the Rattler — '

'We make you sheriff and you declare me no longer an outlaw — '

'An' we all live happily ever afterwards.'

Then Bonnie stopped smiling, because she knew the odds were against their plans maturing as easily as all that. She dreaded the thought of Big M'Grea riding up to those sullen, vengeful Apaches in the hills.

He was moving across to his horse, impatient now to get away. She rose and followed. But he didn't mount for a few seconds; he stood with his chin resting on his saddle, far away in thought. He spoke before putting his boot into the stirrup.

'Thar's jes' one thing, Bonnie. We've got ter make sure we do keep the settlers determined ter wipe out the Laramies as well as the Injuns.' He paused, perhaps looking back into an eventful past. 'I know men; I know how they feel. They'll lick the Injuns — '

'There's a big maybe attached to that, too, by all accounts,' broke in Bonnie.

'Shore. All right, ef they lick the Injuns they'll all turn when that's done an' skedaddle back home as quick as they can. They'll want ter catch up with the work that's been a-pilin' up while they were away, an' after that it's goin' ter be difficult ter get 'em ter come together agen ter lick the Laramies.'

'In fact, we'll be right back where we started. So what, big cowboy? Where do we go from here? And what did you mean about me riding into the Indian country with you?'

He answered her last question.

'You're not safe here, but I don't reckon no harm'll come ter you up among the settlers. They don't like Louen, most of 'em, an' I guess they won't turn you over ter him. Jes' keep back from the fightin' an' you'll be safe.'

Bonnie climbed into her saddle, but she was quiet, thinking. She wasn't as sure as Big M'Grea that she'd be safe among the settlers. Because they were all fighting the Red Man didn't make them angels, and some of the younger fellows were a wild lot.

They rode out of the arroyo and went circling into the scrub country, well away from the trails. It was coming dusk now, and in an hour they would have difficulty in finding their way through the rough bush.

Big M'Grea set the pace with a quick gallop that ate up the miles. He wanted to circle Dead End and come out on the west trail beyond. He had a feeling that west of the town was country safe from the Laramies and the crazy, blue-eyed sheriff and his posse, while down river was enemy territory. He feared the Indians far less at the moment than his white enemies.

Shortly after dark they walked out on to the dirt trail that climbed parallel with the Rio Colorado, quietly murmuring to their left as it tumbled down towards the distant Gulf of Mexico.

After a brief halt they went loping steadily towards the Indian country. Neither spoke. Neither felt like conversation because they were tired from their long day's activities, and then again the rhythmic movement of horseflesh beneath them, the *clud-clud, clud-clud* of unshod hoofs on the soft trail, had a lulling effect. They rode almost asleep in the saddle, as born horsemen do.

About three hours later Big M'Grea pulled up and stiffly dismounted.

'We'll hole up fer the rest of the night,' he told her. 'We might get mistook fer Injuns, an' I shore would hate ter git a bullet in my hide from my friends.'

They didn't unsaddle because there was always the chance they might need to make a quick getaway. M'Grea hobbled the horses Indian fashion, a foreleg to a hind leg, because that way kept them moving in a circle around them — a horse hobbled by its forelegs alone could yet cover a surprising distance in a night.

They eased down into the sandy soil, still warm from the day's hot sun. A stir of breeze moved over them as they lay there under the soft night sky, but they never noticed it, never heard the murmurs of night insects and hunting birds. Sleep came to their tired bodies almost the instant they stretched on the ground.

The world was stirring when M'Grea pulled her to her feet. She came awake at once. She climbed sleepily into the saddle and then the trek began again. She slept for a couple of hours, until the heat of the day was too much for her, and then she pulled herself upright and watched M'Grea as he rode just ahead.

They had cut across a bend of the river, and were riding in desert dust. But she could see his objective — a green valley that was probably the place where the Court rancho lay.

Court rancho, a former Mexican *estancia*, didn't appear to be as badly affected as she had thought might be the case, but its thick adobe walls had provided good protection for the defenders.

There were men about the place here. She could see them on the distant horizon, acting as sentries against sudden attack, while around the rancho they were attending to their equipment, seeing to their injuries, and in general just passing the time until the expected Indian attack developed.

Men looked up from the shade of the wall where they were resting on their bright Mexican blankets and nodded to the big bounty man. They looked curiously at the Mexican boy on the big bay gelding who rode with him, none of them recognizing her, though she was known to many.

As they dismounted Bonnie received a shock. Descending the rancho steps were two men, talking. One she recognized as David Court, the owner of the ranch.

The other was a man who was consulting a red-leather notebook in his hand, a man with an unpleasant nasal accent and nice dude riding pants.

The Easterner.

Bonnie whispered quickly to M'Grea. 'That's the fellow — the Yankee I told you about. What's he doing here, I wonder?'

She was looking at that notebook — it fascinated her. She felt that it contained some secret highly important to the settlers in this valley.

Court called cheerfully: 'Hello, there, you bounty man!' It seemed that M'Grea was already known to them and was on good terms with the fighters.

The greeting caused the Easterner to lift his head, and he saw Bonnie. She knew instantly that he recognized her, for his eyes never left her.

He smiled and lounged across.

'You Mexican boys shore get around,' he said pleasantly.

Bonnie smiled.

'You know very well I'm no Mexican,' she said. 'We don't need to pretend that any longer. You know I'm — '

He lifted his hand quickly. Suddenly she realized that in spite of his quaint manner and unpleasant-sounding speech he was well-intentioned, whatever else he was up to with that mysterious red notebook of his.

He said: 'I don't want to know. I can't even afford to know, d'you understand? You see, as a law-abidin' man, if I knew too much maybe I might have to hand someone over to a mighty unpleasant sheriff I've met. Savvy?'

Bonnie savvied and nodded her head to show it.

'All the same,' she said softly, 'thanks for warning me back there. It certainly helped.'

The Easterner nodded, as if accepting a deep compliment, but made no reply to it. Instead, he shook hands with Court, climbed on to his horse, and rode away.

Bonnie wheeled on David Court.

'Who is that man, Mr Court? And what's he doing around Dead End?'

Court seemed to look hard at her for a moment and then said: 'You don't know? Then you're not goin' ter git ter know from me, Miss Hayday. His business hyar ain't nothin' ter spread around fer all ter know about.'

He was friendly but firm, but his manner only served to make the Easterner all the more mysterious to the girl, and she felt impatient with the ranch owner and was inclined to argue with him.

Then Big M'Grea took her arm and

spoke quietly behind her.

'Take a look around, Mexican boy.'

Startled, Bonnie looked quickly about her. She saw men smiling at her — young men, the Don Juans of the district.

Dismayed, she realized that the Easterner had drawn attention to her, though it had been their intention to be quiet about her identity as long as a possible. Now it seemed that everyone had recognized Bonnie Hayday under that Mexican sombrero.

Those troubled thoughts recurred to her, the doubts she had had yesterday when Big M'Grea had said so optimistically: 'You'll be safe up among the settlers.' Or words to that effect.

Looking into those quick, bright faces under broad-brimmed hats, Bonnie knew that her doubts were justified. This was no place for any girl on her own. In no time they'd be a-wooing her, and then they'd fall to squabbling among themselves. There'd be trouble, and most of it would fall upon Bonnie Hayday, she knew.

She thought, with a touch of humour, 'Where am I to go to be safe?' Then she looked at Big M'Grea, and knew she would be safe while ever she was with him.

M'Grea was speaking to David Court. 'Guess I'd like to have words with you an' the Fighting Committee,' he said.

Court looked shrewdly at the big puncher.

'You got some idea in that big head of your'n, bounty man?'

'Mebbe.'

Court nodded, as if satisfied that his time wouldn't be wasted. He looked across the cool, flagged courtyard, with its roof of vines where a well wall reared at one end of the house proper. He said:

'Looks like some of the committee is in session right now. Playin' poker!'

They strolled across to where a group of five men lay against their saddles under the climbing vines. Court stood over them while they looked up from their cards.

'The bounty man opins ter talk ter you, I reckon,' he said, then he squatted down among them to listen.

M'Grea came to the point immediately.

'We'll never lick this mob of Injuns without help. And back in them hills is a tribe of Apaches that shore don't like the guts o' them Comanches. I know where they are, an' I guess they're nigh on starvin' right now. I reckon mebbe of we offer 'em food they'll jine in the fight agen the blamed Comanches.'

They weren't playing cards now. Eyes looked speculatively up at the big bounty man. There was little optimism in them.

'Who's goin' ter parley with them 'paches?' queried one of the committee.

'Me,' said M Grea laconically.

'You're welcome ter the job.'

The committee man nodded, but, all the same, he didn't try to dissuade M'Grea from the dangerous plan. They were up against it, and anything that looked like a chance of defeating the Comanche was a trick worth trying to take.

But M'Grea had more to say than that.

'Yeah, I'll go, but I'm darned ef I see why I should risk my life jes' ter save the skins of some no-good *hombres* that's doin' nothin' better than nurse cows right now.'

They knew what he meant. One man threw in his cards expressively.

'We've bin talkin' about the Laramies,' he growled. 'We hate their guts, but what c'n we do about it? They won't fight, an' we can't go back an' make 'em fight. They're leavin' us ter do the fightin' for 'em, an' they're quite willin' to have it that way.'

'More than willin' — that's how they want it.' That was another committee man. 'They're holin' up on the south bank of the river, making themselves so safe even the Comanches won't be able ter git across at 'em. An' when it's all over, I reckon they'll be strong enough ter take over any land that ain't got no owner.'

'Guess thar'll be a mighty lot o' land like that when the Comaches is through with us,' growled the first committee man despondently.

Big M'Grea squatted down among them and talked patiently for a while. 'All right, but I figger thar's a way of settlin' scores with the Laramies. I figger this fightin' committee should become a citizens' vigilance committee, just like Bonnie here, Alf York, an' others tried ter raise. An' the way I figger it, the vigilance committee should send back a proclamation ter Dead End sayin' that any man who refuses ter jine in the fight agen the Comanches now has no right to land in the valley hereafter.'

'That's quite an idea,' interposed David Court abruptly. 'It's just, anyway.' They hated the Laramie mob with a burning, savage hatred, and now that there was talk of retribution, it appealed to them. 'No fight — no rights as citizens!'

'But it won't make the Laramies come out, fer all that,' said a committee man cynically. 'They'll laugh at proclamations. An' afterwards, when the fightin's over, they'll be able ter laugh at any of us who survive it.'

There was silence after that, a silence that was broken by M'Grea again.

'Mebbe. But ef I c'n git them Apaches in ter help us, mebbe we'll come out o' the fight pretty strong. All right, while we're strong I'd like ter see the settlers walk back ter the Laramies an' pay 'em out in their own coin.'

Court sighed. 'The idea will work only if you are successful, son. It all depends on you, an' it's a mighty tough task you've set yourself.'

M'Grea rose, satisfied. 'You do your part, I'll do my best with them Apaches. Make the men here realize that the fight's not over when the Injuns is licked. Keep 'em good an' fightin'-mad afterwards, so they'll not start ter

walk away from the big-bellied Laramies. Let's clean up this valley once an'
fer all.' He suddenly looked up at
Bonnie. 'I reckon mebbe I'll be stayin'
around this place fer a long time ter
come.'

'Then we'll be needin' a new sheriff,'
someone interposed drily. 'You won't
live long with Jed Louen a-gunnin' fer
you, an' he shore hates your guts.'

M'Grea merely nodded, as if the
information wasn't either new or
important to him. He said: 'Guess I'll
be goin'. Them Injuns might open
attack agen any time — today, tomorrow. Mighty soon, anyway.'

He filled his bottle at the well and got
some food from David Court's kitchen.
When he got back to his horse he found
that Bonnie had been watering both
beasts and had rubbed them down.
Some of the young sparks were already
trying to talk to her, and were getting a
bit crude with their humour.

They shut up when M'Grea
approached, maybe figuring he had

some greater interest in the girl than they, but he just ignored them. Probably his mind had thoughts only for his hazardous trip into the new Apache territory.

As he swung into his saddle he saw Bonnie mount her horse. 'I'll ride out part of the way with you,' she said carelessly, a shade too carelessly if he had been noticing. So they rode off together, with a lot of 'Good luck, pardner!' shouts from the men.

Up on the ridge M'Grea stopped where he could see right out to the broken foothills of the Edwards Plateau wherein massed the dreaded Comanche raiders. But the great intervening mesquite between seemed devoid of life, save for a few small bunches of stray cattle.

M'Grea sighed his relief. 'That gives us a chance,' he said. 'It don't look like they're goin' ter attack today — ef they had intended ter fight, I reckon they'd have been out ridin' by this time, for sure.'

Half an hour later, climbing among the pines by a track that ran due north, M'Grea seemed to realize that Bonnie was still with him. He drew rein.

'Time you went back, Bonnie,' he smiled. 'You don't need ter go no further.'

So Bonnie told him quite firmly what was in her mind. 'I'm coming with you, right up to the Apache country.' And when he opened his mouth to argue, she went on quickly with her explanation. 'I'm not stayin' back there among the settlers, Tom. Didn't you see the way Lee Dacy was looking at me? And Brad Lorrigan an' other young fellows like them? What sort of a time would I have, d'you think, back there without you to look after me?'

He was worried. 'Shore, I hadn't thought of that. An' back around Dead End thar's that sher'f an' crooked posse, an mebbe the Laramie mob ter help out. It shore is a pickle, Bonnie.'

'It shore is, cowboy,' she mimicked. 'So I reckon there's only one thing for me to do — keep going along with you.'

'But you can't risk your life with them Apaches. You don't know what you're takin' on.'

'Seems like you do, Tom,' she said softly. Then she began to plead. 'Tom, I want to be with you as long as I can. I won't do anything foolhardy, I promise. When we get near the Apaches, I'll hang behind. If things — go wrong' — her voice seemed to catch a little — 'I'll be able to ride back an' tell the committee to forget about help from the Apaches.'

But still he stared at her, his face troubled. So she kicked heels into her horse and settled it by leading the way along the pine crest. 'I'm going,' he heard her voice float back. 'I'm safer for a time with you, Tom, than anywhere. So — let's go!'

They climbed steadily, especially in the late afternoon.

M'Grea said that once on the opposite watershed they'd be able to see the Apache camp far in the valley below — that is, if they hadn't moved on again. He reckoned they'd still be there, though, because further north still was pretty nearly all desert, with very little food and water for the tribe.

They had to pull their horses over the brow because the soil was stony and shifted treacherously underfoot, but immediately on the other side there was plenty of vegetation to give them cover.

They walked their horses into it and let them graze while they clambered across to where a great rocky prow jutted out over the valley, giving them a view of the whole terrain. Panting, they came at last to the end and looked over. She heard M'Grea's almost instant sigh of relief.

'They're there — still there?'

He pointed them out to her — a cluster of tepees where a small river wound in the dark green of the valley bottom. She saw braves and squaws walking between the tents, saw the papooses playing, and heard the Apache dogs snarling and fighting.

Her heart grew cold, for this was the time of parting.

M'Grea looked at the sun, only two hours above the horizon. 'I'd better start movin',' he said suddenly. 'I want to come openly up to that camp.' He shrugged. 'That's the only way I c'n git ter talk to them alive, I reckon.' Bonnie followed. Just about to mount, she heard his voice say gruffly, 'Don't kid yourself you're altogether safe up here, Bonnie. Keep your eyes skinned fer them varmints, an' git as far back along the trail as you can afore sundown. That is, ef you have ter go back without me.'

Bonnie was crying at his elbow. He must have heard her, for he turned and looked down into her weeping face. She couldn't move, couldn't avert her face from his — just stood and looked up at him, while her heart broke and the tears streamed out her unhappiness.

'Oh, Tom,' she whispered, and her voice was a wail of anguish, 'just when I was getting to know you. Just when I was getting to like you. Now you have to go and — and maybe I'll never see you again.'

She broke down completely at that, head suddenly bowed as her sobs shook her slim body. She felt his big, strong arms come soothingly round to hold her and comfort her, heard his gentle, confident drawl — 'Guess I've got my own opinion on that, Bonnie. Guess I'm goin' ter turn in the Rattler an' Dutch George ter justice yet, you see ef I don't!'

But she knew he was saying it to comfort her, knew that even he didn't think much to his chances.

'It's the only way, I suppose,' she whispered, turning to wipe her tears. It was what pioneers had to do when a community that included women and children was in danger. Single, independent men like big Tom M'Grea had to take appalling risks in an effort to save their fellows.

'Yes, I must go. Goodbye — honey!' For a moment she thought he was going to kiss her, and then he pulled himself away and heaved himself into his saddle with one quick movement. 'Goodbye,' he called again, then he sent his horse sliding like a big black cat down the steep mountain slopes.

She didn't weep any more, but climbed once again out on to that rocky spur and watched him all the way down. And all the way she was saying to herself, 'He called me honey! Tom M'Grea called me honey! Oh, heaven, please let him come out of this alive!'

For Tom M'Grea was the only man she had ever met whom she wanted to call her by a term of endearment such as honey.

It took him half an hour to get down to the camp, but long before he reached it she could see that his approach had been detected. There was a lot of scurrying about among the tepees, and then the braves began to mass just outside the lines of tents to await the solitary rider's approach. Back of them the squaws and their papooses watched apprehensively.

Bonnie's heart was clutched by some cold, icy hand as she saw the big bounty man go riding steadily up to that savage, hostile group of brown men. These weren't the Apaches who hung around the settlements, poor, degenerate types; these were the Apaches of the plains, primitive, untutored and everlusting for blood. Anything might happen as she watched, and she feared the worst.

She saw him ride slowly up towards an isolated group that probably contained the chief of the tribe. His hand was raised in friendly greeting.

She saw the braves come suddenly flooding round the lone horseman — saw an arm lift, and a tomahawk strike the bounty man from the saddle.

She screamed and involuntarily raised her hands to her eyes, as if by shutting out the sight so she prevented the deed. But it had happened; she knew it — Big M'Grea of the fighting heart had been treacherously struck down the moment he rode into the Apache camp.

Tears scalding down her cheeks, moaning with grief, she turned blindly back towards her horse. Her head lifted to see her way; her vision cleared.

A brown savage face peered at her from five yards distance.

Half a dozen braves were silently watching her from back among the brush.

She screamed and her hand dived for her Colt but before she could draw it clear a wave of sweaty, near-naked bodies fell on top of her and she was helpless.

* * *

They were watching the northern horizon hopefully next morning when the might of the Comanche army came streaking across the plains to attack the settlers. The wise ones said it was too early to expect anything from M'Grea yet, and the still wiser — or more hopeless — said they never would hear anything more from him. It wasn't to be expected that Apaches would fight alongside their old enemy, the Paleface, even against the savage, murdering Comanche.

Only one voice was raised against that argument. It was David Court's. 'He's got a powerful lever,' he kept saying. 'Thar's no food north fer a big tribe of 'paches, an' even Injuns like ter go on eatin'. Food talks pretty loud sometimes; mebbe it'l bring the 'pache in on our side.' Then he shrugged. 'That is, ef they give the bounty man chance ter open his mouth an' make the offer.'

The Comanches took time to get to the Court Valley. It wasn't the way of Indians to plunge into any carefully planned battle.

A large party decided to ride down to the Rio Colorado and burn out a couple of small settlements that had withstood the first attack. They found them a bit too tough to crack without the main body of Comanche warriors, for the settlers had been joined by many resolute friends from the surrounding district.

After a few fierce but abortive charges, this small section of the Comanches came riding back to rejoin the tribe.

They came on steadily across the mesquite after that, rounding up cattle, setting fire to winter fodder on one isolated holding that had been missed before, and all the time coming nearer to the green Court Valley.

Perhaps they didn't know that this was a defensive line of the white man's. They rode up in a mighty host of a thousand wild braves, until suddenly a crackle of gunfire spat out at them all along the line of the tributary. At once they raised their lances with their fluttering streamers and charged in a great, screaming mass.

They were beaten off, as much as anything because the settlers had lain loose wires all among the grass and the first charge went down in a mêlée of upturned, terrified ponies. And the deadly rifles of the settlers took terrific toll of the enemy.

They went circling back out of range at that, and grouped under a high, wind-eroded sand cliff, where they held conclave. Then back again they charged, this time leaping the trip wires and getting almost within the defences before the settlers' fire grew too hot for them and just when victory was within their grasp the leaders faltered and then rode away.

There was no more wild charging after that. The Comanche had learned his lesson — that it was too expensive to ride openly on to the white man's repeating rifles. They left their horses well to the rear and came stealing closer, taking advantage of any cover that the prairie offered.

But that slow approach, with its certainty of victory at the end of it, didn't start until well into the afternoon, and by that time the settlers had stopped thinking of any help coming from M'Grea and the Apaches.

David Court was the last to give up hope. He took a final glance at the northern hills and said, 'Guess M'Grea didn't have no luck — an' that poor gal, too. She musta rode with him an' got herself caught. He had guts, that bounty man — plenty guts.'

Then he opened long range fire on the first wave of dismounted attackers.

They had reckoned that if the Apaches were coming to help at all they would have arrived long before noon; because clearly M'Grea would have brought them over the mountains during the night. Now it was late in the afternoon —

Alf York came out on a wagon with Coogan, Kurt Reimer and a few other old-timers. They told of the reception that the new-formed Vigilance Proclamation had had when it was posted up in Dead End.

One of the old Fighting Committee had carried it down. He had stuck it up on the Wells Fargo freight board, then he'd ridden off to deliver a similar proclamation to the Laramies personally.

A crowd had gathered, mostly old men, a lot of women, and a few squalling children.

'Louen's dep'ties was whar they've bin most o' the time you people have bin fightin',' old Alf explained bitterly. 'Drinkin' an' gamblin' an' havin' a right roysterin' time in Milligan's. We could hear the noise whar we lay cooped up in that danged prison the Laramies made fer Louen.'

But Louen had come out of his office, attracted by the gathering crowd. He had lounged across to read the proclamation, and then he had stood back, that crazy laughter in his blue eyes, his teeth showing clean and white and even in his good-looking, boyish face. He had stood and smiled and silently challenged anyone to speak about the matter to him.

Someone at the back had grown bold

and shouted, 'Why don't you go an' take your drunken, murderin' dep'ties with you, sher'f?'

Louen had mocked them. His skin was so thick that words couldn't hurt him. 'What, an' leave you old critters an' your womenfolk at the mercy of the Injuns when they come a-ridin' through?'

Just as plainly he could have told them that he had no intention of turning Indian fighter when it was so much more comfortable here around the Dead End saloon. Just as plainly he could have jeered, 'You suckers c'n do the fightin' for me!' And they knew it.

His tough, two-gun posse was grouping around him, ready to go into action if need showed even slightly. But the people there were old; they were no match for professional gunmen. So wisely they looked their hate but kept it off their tongues.

Alf York and his companions, clinging to the bars of their cell, had heard everything. So Alf had called, 'Sher'f

Louen, goldarn it, let us outa this crib so's we c'n go up an' take a smack at them danged redskins.'

It had been a forlorn appeal, and yet it had succeeded. Jed Louen had considered it for a second, and then suddenly he nodded. 'Shore, why not?' he smiled. It was the smile of death. 'Reckon mebbe them Injuns might save me an unpleasant job at some time.' And he had lounged carelessly across and released them.

'We ain't much of fightin' men,' smiled the old storekeeper, 'but mebbe we'll knock down a few red 'uns afore they put an arrow into my big belly.'

An hour later the committeeman who had borne the message to the Circle ranch also came riding in. They were now under close siege from the lines of Indians sniping at them from the cover less than a hundred yards away.

One look at the proclamation bearer's face was enough.

'The three Laramies took it as a joke. They tore up the proclamation right under my nose and told me to beat it or they'd make li'l pieces outa me, too. They said they weren't fightin' for nobody else's property. They could hold their own agen any redskins and that's all that concerned them.'

He licked his lips, remembering back. He was a dry-looking, sour-stick of an old-timer, and just now he was hating the Laramie mob.

'They also said that what they owned they held, and there warn't enough people up this valley ter say they couldn't own any land 'cause they didn't foller the Fightin' Committee agen the redskins.'

They turned away at that and vented their hating hearts on the approaching Comanches. Now they were beginning to lose defenders fast, though as yet most arrows and bullets that found targets wounded rather than killed.

The committeeman had just one other subject to mention.

'There was some mighty interestin' people sittin' out with the Laramies when I rode up. Two of 'em were those fellars that bounty man tried ter take in. I reckon Burt Laramie's offered pertection if they tote their guns fer him.'

'And the other?' David Court was asking the question, because the committeeman was looking rather queerly in his direction.

'It was that danged Easterner, him with the fancy pants. He seemed in right good spirits with the Laramies, sittin' there within' in his li'l red book.'

David Court said nothing at that, but turned thoughtfully away — very thoughtful.

Then the attack really opened up. It came when the settlers realized that they'd had all the reinforcements they were likely to get from Dead End and district.

Court pulled trigger until his rifle grew so hot he thought the barrel would bend. And he thought, 'How much longer can we hold 'em off? Half an hour — or five more minutes?' And he thought the latter estimate might be the more accurate one. His face was haggard, weary. It wasn't a good way to go out after all those brave pioneering days, those days of rich young hopes . . .

12

War Talk

Big M'Grea came slowly up to the Apaches, ignoring the lowering, sullen looks. He raised his hand on high to show it was empty of weapon and that he came in peace.

He knew little of the Apache tongue, but he guessed that some here would know English, so he called, 'How, Red Brother. I come in peace.' Suddenly the braves came flooding round him, weapons raised threateningly. He looked down on a jostling mass of brown bodies, of lean, copper-bronze arms lifted so that they looked like a writhing sea of serpents.

He called again, shouting for the distant knot of chiefs to hear.

'Peace, O Apache warriors! I come to talk of war against the Comanche, of the food you can get from us — '

Someone dealt him a stunning blow from behind and he toppled down into eager hands that waited to rend the white enemy. The blow was hard, but he never really lost consciousness. He felt hands rip his shirt from his back, knew that his guns had been plucked from their holsters.

Then madly he struggled to his feet, but once there he found he was helpless within the press of surging, sweaty brown bodies. Yet perhaps the very fierceness with which they pressed against him saved his life; for so close were they, they could not find room in which to swing a weapon again.

Bleeding from the head wound and naked to his waist, Big M'Grea was dragged across towards the tepees. He had time to think 'This is whar I git my pass-out check,' and to feel glad that he had left Bonnie well away from the camp. He wondered what she would do when she saw what was happening to him, and he thought of her tears — for he knew she would weep for him.

Then the press parted before him and he looked upon the foulest thing he had ever seen.

It was the medicine man.

He was so old he looked like a withered apple — just a bundle of shrivelled skin that hung loosely about his uncertain bones. His face was painted blue, and about his head were the coils of a mighty rattlesnake that hadn't been properly cured and stank to high heaven. Hanging from his wrists were wings torn from buzzards, the blood barely congealed at the tips, while his body was adorned with the raw pelts of many small animals.

In revulsion M'Grea tried to draw back from the threatening apparition. Then the ancient medicine man came fluttering nearer, his voice a scream that sounded like a death sentence to the cowboy.

Yet he felt the hands slacken about him, felt their clutches fade and the arms drop away so that he was free.

272

Free, though surrounded by hostile Indians.

And the medicine man was jabbering, gesticulating, pointing to the new pelts that adorned his body and then to M'Grea. The bounty man didn't know it, but the medicine man was calling, 'My medicine has worked. See, I have made the Big Talk with the Great Spirit. To him I made the sacrifices of all small things that inhabit the prairie and I asked him for bigger game in order that our empty bellies should be filled. And the Great Spirit has answered me. The Great Spirit has sent this white man to lead us to the food!'

M'Grea was not to know it, but the medicine man's stock had fallen with a bang with the rout of the Apaches by their Comanche enemies. There were some wicked spirits in that tribe who held medicine men in less revere than they ought to have done; and those voices had begun to speak loudly and to be awkward in the last week or so.

He had been an uneasy medicine

man right until M'Grea had ridden into camp and shouted out the word 'food.' Now he was taking his chances, that medicine man; for if M'Grea could bring food to them, then he, the medicine man, would take credit for it.

Plainly, what he was saying had effect upon the hundreds of Indians who crowded in close circle around the prisoner. The chiefs and lesser chiefs had pushed their way through the throng and were listening intently, and when someone seemed about to raise a hand against the paleface the chief stopped him with a gesture.

M'Grea began to realize that he had been given a reprieve, but it didn't warm his heart towards that repulsive medicine man, even so.

The medicine man spoke in a cracked old voice in an English gathered in his youth around the early Texas settlements.

'You spik of food. The Great Spirit sends you to lead us to food, huh?'

Big M'Grea took his clue.

'The Great Spirit sends me to lead my red brothers to plenty food. But the Great Spirit says you must first fight the danged Comanches alongside the white man. A war party of fine, brave Apaches could be waitin' in them hills, an' when the Comanches go ridin' east agen the settlers, the Apaches could burn the Comanche village an' drive all the womenfolk an' old people right back into the hills.'

That was the best plan he had figgered out, and it seemed the only one likely to attract the Apache in his present mood. M'Grea knew that if it were entered upon it would save the situation so far as the settlers were concerned.

When the Comanches knew that their womenfolk were being attacked — and their burning village would tell them that — they would break off the battle with the white man in order to go to their rescue. If the white man was smart he would ride after the Comanches and would do such damage with his long-range guns that the invader would be in no condition to resume war against the settlers or even the Apaches for a long time to come.

M'Grea knew that the idea appealed to the Apaches by the way they murmured quickly and excitedly at his words.

Then his friend, the stinking medicine man, came and shoved his ugly face close to the puncher's. 'That food, white man. When do we get it, huh?'

M'Grea said, 'We'll give you five wagon loads of grain — our biggest wagons.' He knew he could promise that on behalf of the settlers. Then he clinched the deal by adding, 'And a thousand head o' cattle will be given to you, too.' And he knew where he was going to get the cattle!

They sat and discussed it, murmuring and talking, and sometimes getting excited about what they were saying. And then suddenly the decision was made for the wary braves.

The hungry squaws in the background joined in with wails and lamentful cries and held their papooses up to show how thin they had become for lack of food.

M'Grea knew then that he had won the Apaches over to him. At last a brave-interpreter told him they would ride against the Comanches. Not, he was at pains to point out, directly against the tribe, but only as M'Grea had suggested against the Comanche village in the absence of the warriors.

M'Grea got to his feet. That Comanche village was a long ride away and he wanted to start immediately and be in a position to attack at first light. But the Apaches, for all their hunger, didn't like moving in the dark.

They feared the Evil Spirits, they said, but at length M'Grea won them over on that point, too. In the end they said they would ride through the night but not fight during the dark hours.

It satisfied the bounty man, and he

rose while the braves went among their tepees to get food and drink before starting, and see to their guns and other weapons.

M'Grea strolled around the camp, making himself as conspicuous as possible. He wanted Bonnie to see him, so that she could carry back the tidings to the settlers that he appeared to be meeting with success on his mission. But he didn't dare signal to her in case the touchy, suspicious Apaches suspected a plot against them.

He didn't know that while he walked about the Indian camp, head throbbing from that tomahawk blow, still shirtless though he had got his guns back, Bonnie Hayday was lying unconscious over the back of a pony that was ridden by a savage Comanche.

They started out after dark, over four hundred grim, vengeful Apaches. Nearly half their number were without horses, but this was little handicap to nimble men with that hilly country intervening.

Scouts were sent out a far way ahead and along their flanks, while the main body of Apaches rode and ran between. A thin crescent of moon came up that night, to reveal a long, snaky column of silent Indians filing their way on to the long, pine-crested saddleback that was like a bridge across to the distant foothills of the Edwards plateau.

As they came nearer to the enemy-held territory, however, the progress of the nervous Apaches grew much slower, greatly to the exasperation of the bounty man. There were frequent stops and long, grunting conversations, while reports from their scouts were heard.

They were still miles from the Comanche village when, two hours before dawn, a scout came sliding back to warn them of danger. They froze into the darkness of a long hillside that was covered with stunted oaks and black-thorn.

Suddenly, silhouetted against the paling night sky, they saw the plumed headdress of a Comanche appear along the ridge top. In a minute there were hundreds silently riding across the ridge before them.

The Comanches were already out on the warpath!

After that they saw party after party of Comanches go riding east towards the Court tributary and the line held by that small band of resolute pioneers.

The Apaches refused to move at all in the dark now, and perhaps they were wise because the countryside ahead of them seemed alive with red enemies, who were in vastly superior strength.

Even when dawn came, there was a long wait until the scouts were sure of the way ahead. Then the slow, cautious march was resumed.

The nearer they came to the Comanche village the slower their pace. M'Grea watched the sun rise until his shadow barely covered his boot toes, and then it began the long descent towards the western horizon. He kept listening, trying to hear sounds of fighting back east, but the distance must have been too great, for he heard nothing.

It was late in the afternoon before they were in a position over that valley in which lay the Comanche village — almost in that identical position where M'Grea had lain once before with his two prisoners. They peered down cautiously and saw a vast town of buffalo-hide tents on crossed tepee poles.

Before anyone could give a signal, they went over the top in a mad, screaming horde of vengeful warriors. M'Grea rode in behind, sickened at the thought of the slaughter that was to come. However, he had reckoned without the Comanche braves who had been left behind to guard the village. True to their training as the bravest of all Indians, they came riding out to take on this overwhelming army of Apaches.

They hadn't a chance, and all those Comanches knew it, but they came out to fight and buy time so that their womenfolk could escape with the children.

The Comanches fought a desperate rearguard battle, giving ground only when the mass was too great and flung them back. Their numbers dwindled, but they never gave in, and it took the Apaches all of half an hour before they finally defeated them and were able to ride in savage triumph up to the Comanche village.

It was deserted. The hardy squaws, true wives of a warrior folk, were miles away by then up the rocky trails that led to the vastnesses of the great Staked Plains. M'Grea, watching them flit swiftly up the roughest mountain trails thought, 'They'll never catch 'em now,' and he felt glad.

Fighting red men was one thing; killing women and children was another and one he couldn't contemplate without nausea.

The Comanche camp was quickly plundered. It was coming close on to evening now. Then the exultant

Apaches behaved as he had expected them to behave — they set fire to their enemy's dwellings and a great pillar of smoke rose to heaven as a witness to their act of revenge.

* * *

Faraway to the west, unexpectedly the gunfire dwindled against the white men. Just when it seemed that the Comanche attack must succeed and within minutes they would be overrun and slaughtered, the Comanche onslaught slackened and then mysteriously petered out.

David Court's warning voice rang out:

'Don't be taken in. This might be a blamed Injun ruse!'

But it was no ruse, and within seconds they all knew it. The settlers began to stand up behind their defences, suddenly delirious with joy. 'We've licked 'em!' they shouted. 'They're takin' their hosses an' runnin' away!'

They were. The Comanches were racing for their bare-backed ponies, leaping on to them and going back across the mesquite in a mad, headlong gallop.

Then someone shouted, 'Look thar!' And they looked far back into the foothills, where a great column of smoke poured up towards the setting sun.

They understood at once what had happened.

'It's that bounty hunter, M'Grea,' they shouted. 'He's led an attack on the Comanche village, and them pesky varmints is off ter put a stop to it.'

And then they cheered M'Grea, cheered and cheered him. For it was as they imagined, the big bounty hunter was responsible for saving them all from slaughter. Right then they'd have voted for M'Grea as President, he was so popular with the delighted, joyous settlers.

But David Court brought them back to earth. 'We got ter rub it in,' he shouted. 'After them Injuns an' teach 'em a lesson. To horse!'

'To horse!' went the cry right down their line as far as the broad Rio Colorado, and within seconds eighty of them, all that were left who were still capable of clinging to a saddle, were charging in the wake of the retreating Comanches.

Back by the burning village M'Grea guessed what was happening across the plains towards the west. He called to the chiefs, shouting that they should pull out without delay, in case returning Comanches caught up with them. It sounded good advice, and the chiefs signalled for the Apaches to return with their plunder.

M'Grea watched them file past, some laden with spoil from the tents, a few leading horses that had been captured.

One was a bay gelding. It had saddle and bridle that had never been made by an Indian. In sudden horror M'Grea spurred across to it. When he came up he knew he hadn't made any mistake.

This was Bonnie Hayday's horse!

Madly M'Grea went spurring around the village, looking everywhere for the girl or for traces of her, asking questions of every Indian that he saw. But there was no trace, and no Apache had seen his white squaw.

He came back to where they had prisoners, a few wounded who had been captured alive. M'Grea questioned them, and he knew their language fairly well. At first they didn't speak, and then one, perhaps deliberately trying to hurt their white enemy, sneered: 'White man's squaw was left tied in tepee. White man set fire to Comanche tepee. White man's squaw she burn plenty fast, huh?'

M'Grea drew back, sickened. He looked at the blazing tepees. There was no one alive among them now. All the same, he lingered, calling in the hope that somehow a voice would answer him. But none came.

A mile down river, however, he found a frightened settler's horse with its head harness caught up in a bush, and when he had released it he swopped mounts because it was fresher, and he made good time down to the Court tributary and then up to David Court's ranch.

It was dark when he came up, and he was challenged by lookouts. When they saw who it was they nearly tore his arm off in their delight, and their shouts brought everyone running down to greet him. It was a proud moment for M'Grea — that is, it should have been.

But all he could think of was Bonnie Hayday lying bound in a blazing tepee while he sat his horse unknowingly perhaps only a hundred yards away.

He fell wearily out of his saddle in the flagged courtyard at the Court ranch house. The men gathered round, asking questions, telling him how they had gone on.

They had pursued the Comanches for a full half-hour, dealing out incredible slaughter to their fleeing, suddenly routed foes, and then they had returned so as not to be caught out on the wide prairie away from their defence line.

'I guess it'll be a long time afore them pesky Comanches'll have strength ter pick a fight with the white man agen,' said David Court happily.

Then M'Grea asked with his last remaining hope: 'Anyone seen Bonnie Hayday?' But no one had.

M'Grea told the men what he had promised the Indians. They said, 'Shore, shore,' when he told them of the five wagonloads of corn promised. David Court said: 'I'll send the first waggon out at dawn ter let 'em see we intend ter keep our promises.'

But when M'Grea said he had also promised a thousand head of cattle, they looked at him as if he had gone mad. 'A thousand head — fer Injuns?' They looked at each other, and the thought in their minds was, 'Who's goin' ter give 'em the cattle?'

Corn they would give willingly, but it was against all their instincts as cattlemen to part with valuable stock that were needed to build up their herds. Cattle was their life — to give away such a number to Indians sounded the height of folly.

'Wal, ef you promised 'em,' began David Court uneasily, and then the bounty hunter stopped him.

'I didn't promise 'em your cattle. Court. When I made that promise I decided whar to get the cattle, too — from the Laramie mob. Why not? They won't need any any more. They wouldn't fight the Injuns, so I reckon they're not entitled ter any land along this valley.'

He looked round the circle of faces illuminated by a flickering log fire in the courtyard. His own was hard — hard to cover the aching softness of his breaking heart just then.

'Yeah, I did that deliberately. I didn't want you ter fergit the Laramies when the fightin' was over with the Comanches. I promised the Apaches some Laramie cattle ter make you go in an' take 'em from the varmints.

Now you've got ter take action agen the Laramies.'

'It might be less expensive to give the Apaches some of our own cattle,' interposed one settler wearily. 'We've had enough of fightin', M'Grea. We can't all go ridin' off to the Circle ranch with your demands, bounty man. That wouldn't be safe. Most of us'll have ter stay an' keep watch in case them red varmints come back — mebbe we'll be lyin' around the Court Valley fer a week or two until they clear off into the hills agen.'

There was a growl of assent from the settlers. The red enemy always came first. They weren't inclined to move against the Laramies while there was a red warrior as near to them as the foothills of the plateau.

But Alf York heaved his bulk into the firelight just then. He spoke slowly, a fat old man who had spent most of his life serving groceries across a counter; and yet a courageous old man, a man in whom the fine, brave pioneering spirit still ran strongly.

'Guess you don't need me no more, fellars. Guess thar's enough o' you hyer ter take care o' them pesky Injuns — though I reckon myself they'll never come back after terday's awful tannin'.' He looked into the fire, his face heavy with thought. 'I'm goin' back ter Dead End tomorrow.' His face suddenly lifted pugnaciously. 'Only I ain't gonna let no two-timin', crazy sher'f put me behind bars agen.'

Old Coogan said: 'Nor me, neither,' and spat into the fire.

'No, sir. That ain't no life fer me, bein' shoved around by any Laramie stooge. This thing's got ter be settled now, once an' fer all. I'm goin' back ter Dead End with my guns in my hand, even of I have ter go alone.'

Coogan said: 'You'll find me treadin' on your heels, Alf.'

And Kurt Reimer said: 'Ef you don't walk too fast fer my game leg, pards, you'll haff me with you, too.'

'The old-timers, eh?' M'Grea laughed.

There was a fine fighting spirit in these men. 'I'm goin', too. That makes four of us.'

Someone realized that he was still without shirt and threw one across. David Court exclaimed: 'All right, you fire-eaters. Mebbe we c'n watch fer Injuns an' smoke out the Laramies, too. I reckon thar's plenty wounded who can still tote guns. They c'n stay hyar an' shoot up Redskins ef they return. We'll keep mebbe fifty or sixty men, 'cause it shore is a long way down to the Rio.' He sighed and looked round. 'Guess you'll have no more'n forty men at that, Alf.'

'It's enough,' said, the big store-keeper.

'They've got at least sixty agen you — an' professional killers at that, Alf,' Court said warningly.

'We'll get over that somehow,' said the courageous fat man, and then they all went to rest their exhausted bodies in much-needed slumber.

M'Grea got them out of their

blankets long before sunrise, though many protested and a few wanted to change their minds. But M'Grea wanted to be in Dead End before noon, because after cleaning up the sheriff's posse there was still the trek on to the Circle ranch across the river, and that would take time.

He rode in silence with the rest of the men until they came into Dead End.

Half the men flanked out and made a cordon round the town, but M'Grea, Alf York and a dozen others just kept grimly on. This was to be a showdown.

A few people turned out when they heard the advancing hoofs — they were women mostly, and all friendly to the party.

'Whar's Louen an' his gunnies?' demanded Alf York from the heights of his great horse.

They weren't sure. Some said maybe in his office; others said he'd be up at Milligan's, where most of his posse lived. So they continued to the sheriff's new office, where M'Grea swung down and kicked open the door — but Loco Lou wasn't there.

He came back to his horse and mounted and they rode up to the saloon. By now there wasn't a doorway or window without an occupant. The people watched, silent, praying for the safety of their menfolk. And yet knowing that this had to be done.

Just by the saloon an old man with a beard like a goat's that has been caught up in thorns a few times quavered: 'Hey, bounty man, reckon you'll find one o' your fellars inside thar!'

'Who? Dutch George — or the Rattler?' But the old man couldn't say what name the varmint had.

M'Grea swung round in his saddle. His voice was filled with a kind of cold passion.

'Thar's one o' my men inside Milligan's,' he told them. 'I want that critter alive, savvy? An' I'll shoot any *hombre* that tries ter gun him — savvy?'

They savvied. But it didn't make them want to go into that saloon now, with such a handicap against them.

M'Grea went in. They must have just been told that a party was on its way after them, for Rope Coltas and a couple of men were just coming down from the backquarters still buckling on their belts. They halted in the bend of the stairs when M'Grea's big foot kicked open the batwing doors — stopped there, tense and waiting.

M'Grea walked into the room. Alf York suddenly shoved a rifle barrel through a window, and squinted fatly down the sights at the dozen rough-necks at the tables, playing cards even at this early hour of the day.

Still no one moved. Maybe they'd heard they were outnumbered two or three to one and didn't intend to make the first play. But they were watchful, heads lowered, hands poised ready for the dive for their guns — their eyes never blinking in case they lost any advantage in that fraction of a second.

M'Grea crouched just inside the room, the brim of his hat so low that his steely grey eyes barely showed beneath it. He saw the man he was looking for, knew that to call out would precipitate gunplay.

But he called him.

'Dutch George, you low, murderin' swine, I'm back ter take you fer a hangin' at Stampede! Walk out with your hands up, or I'll drag you out!'

Dutch George's face went purple-red above the blue stubble of his puffy face.

'Like hell you'll drag me out!' he shouted recklessly, and went for his guns.

M'Grea's came leaping into his hands; knees bent, he leaped forward, triggering flame as he did so. A bullet spanged into the leather of Dutch George's holster even as he started to draw his gun. The shock caused the gunman to drop the vibrating steel and look to his hand in alarm.

M'Grea's other bullets smashed bottles back of the bar. They didn't harm anyone, but the noise was calculated to cause a minor diversion.

The gunnies dived for cover and came up with guns roaring. They were tough, fighting like cornered rats, but for once they had been taken at a disadvantage. By now a lot of irate citizens were poking in at the windows of Milligan's with pretty lethal weapons. The sawn-off shotguns especially were highly effective in that confined space.

M'Grea had to crawl out without his man because of the flying shotgun pellets. As he came out he took a flesh wound under his right arm, but it was only later that it seemed to get painful.

Outside of the batwings, his guns blazing whenever a target crossed his vision, he called: 'Watch out fer Loco Lou! He don't seem ter be in Milligan's!'

The battle of Milligan's Saloon — that's what the wags called it afterwards — raged for what seemed an eternity but was probably no more than a quarter of an hour. At the end of that time there wasn't a man inside except one without lead somewhere under his skin. That one was Dutch George. Even in the heat of battle the settlers remembered M'Grea's threat and kept their guns to other targets.

There came a point finally when even the gunmen had had enough of their own medicine, and they began to sing out for quarter. M'Grea shouted for them to come out with their hands up, and they started to file painfully, crest-fallenly out. Last to come was Dutch George, evil, tense, and glowering.

They put them all in the new jail to minister to each other's wounds, and then rode off to the Circle ford across the Rio Colorado. It was a good quarter of a mile wide at this point, and when they saw armed sentries patrolling the far bank they halted to discuss tactics.

'There isn't a one of us will get across that river alive,' opined one of the setlers. 'Not with them critters lookin' down their rifles at us!'

They were still sitting their horses on

the north bank, trying to figure out a way of crossing that wide river without being killed, when a lone horseman came riding steadily up to the ford. When M'Grea saw the polished leggings and dude pants' he rode across to intercept the rider.

'Where are you goin', stranger?' he asked, and his voice was barely polite.

The Yankee said: 'It's none of your business; but I'll tell you. I'm crossin' this hyar river in order ter speak ter the owner of that ranch we can see.'

'What makes you think you'll get across alive? We know we can't.'

The Yankee tapped his breast pocket and said nasally: 'I reckon I got somethin' here that'll keep the guns outa their hands while I cross. Goodday, bounty man. Give my regards to Miss Hayday when you see her.'

M'Grea pulled his horse round. 'Miss Hayday died last night in a fire at an Injun camp,' he said, and his voice was toneless because he *had* to keep the emotion out of his voice. More and more he realized how he missed the girl he had known for such a little time —

The Easterner looked genuinely shocked. 'Gee, I'm sorry!' Then he said no more but spurred into the river.

When M'Grea rode back to the settlers he found a good part of them about to quit. They argued doggedly that the Laramies were too strong for them; they held the whip-hand now as always.

M'Grea said impulsively: 'Look, *hombres*, I'll figger out a way of gettin' them critters away from the ford long enough fer you all ter ride across. Will you stay here two — mebbe three — more hours an' see what I c'n do?'

The beginnings of an idea were already simmering in M'Grea's quick mind. He look at the sun. He hadn't much time —

He went away like a whirlwind, leaving a surprised bunch of pioneers to make themselves comfortable in any

shade they could find on that desolat
north bank of the river.

Three hours later they decided tl
nothing was going to happen, but so
of the men said: 'Let's give the fellar
another half-hour,' and they settled
down in the shade once more.

About a quarter of an hour after this
they saw the mounted sentries on the
south bank pull together, confer, and
then all go racing inland.

In a flash they were on their own
horses, driving them into the cool
brown waters. And it was from that
height that they understood what had
happened.

'Apaches!' shouted the settlers, putting spurs to their mounts and riding
hell for leather across to that unguarded
bank.

At the apparent threat of an Indian
attack — probably under the impression that they were the warlike
Comanches, anyway — all the Circle
cowboys had gone racing back to the
cover of the ranch buildings.

They were still there, not understanding the trick that M'Grea had played on them, when the strong party of settlers came galloping up to were M'Grea sat his horse alone on the prairie.

'That shore was a good trick, Bounty Man,' a rancher called.

M'Grea nodded. Nothing — not even success — made him feel enthusiastic then.

'It was easy,' he said. 'I jes' told them Apaches they could have as many Circle cattle as they could drive off. Guess they've got more than the thousand I promised 'em!'

And then the firing began. The irate settlers had many scores to settle and weren't in a mood to think of mercy. There was a long moment of fighting all around the ranch buildings and up between the cattle runs leading out from the corrals. The settlers had their rifles, the Circle men Colts only. And the rifle is a more accurate weapon at more than twenty paces.

M'Grea went riding through, trying to storm into the compound that was built, Spanish fashion, about the ranch-house. His guns flamed and emptied, were reloaded, and began to empty again.

M'Grea went sliding into the cover of a deep, 'dobe doorway, and paused to reload. The sweat ran into his eyes, blinding him. He realized that shooting had started from a balcony above him, and when he turned he saw that his followers had burst open the gates and were beginning to edge into the courtyard.

He went through the doorway. A Mexican came at him suddenly from a sideroom. It was Durango, the gambler, who had come over with Jed Louen that afternoon, but M'Grea didn't know it. The explosions from those Colt cylinders seemed to rock the room, and the bite of gun fumes got into M'Grea's nostrils and made them smart.

For it was M'Grea's Colts that did the firing — Durango who slumped, gun in hand, a corpse in that curtained doorway.

He killed and killed and killed yet again, and then he was on those wide stone stairs that curved to the upper rooms where the balconies were.

He came suddenly out on to them.

And he couldn't understand it, because the settlers were in a throng right out in the open of the courtyard now, and they weren't firing.

Yet here on the balcony were all the enemies that M'Grea seemed ever to have had.

King Rattler. Louen of the crazy blue eyes. Nils Perhof, the gambling man. Big, burly, even now arrogant. Burt Laramie, still cool, still confident he could turn the tables on his enemies. And sitting quite coolly drinking at a white-clothed table was a man with dude pants and a red-leather notebook that was as mysterious as the man himself.

He realized he had the drop on his enemies and his guns began to lift.

They felt like all the weights in hades — he had lost a lot of blood and was spent suddenly. But they were coming up: he'd get some of them before they got him —

Someone shouted in panic down below: 'M'Grea, don't!'

His guns halted in surprise.

'Look who's with them!'

And Bonnie Hayday was standing among them, and jammed into her ribs was a gun held by vicious, conscience-less King Rattler.

Bonnie! A hostage! That's why the vigilantes were holding their fire; why he had been told to hold his. She would die first if he pulled trigger.

Die — But he had thought she was already dead.

M'Grea's eyes switched from the group. He looked straight into the eyes of the Easterner with the dude pants. The Easterner put down his glass.

Something was happening among that group.

Jed Louen, still mockingly smiling in

spite of the danger, could be heard to drawl, 'Looks like we'll get outa hyar alive, Burt, but I reckon you're through in Dead End fer all time.'

'You don't know me, Loco,' said the rancher confidently, and then he stopped, remembering.

'Loco?' Those blue eyes crackled with crazy mirth. 'Nobody calls me — Loco!'

That pause was to bring a gun round. Burt started to fire but missed. Then he was on his knees, clutching his stomach, slumping on to his haunches, suddenly pitching on his face and dying.

And King Rattler was dying with him.

The Easterner grabbed at Bonnie's hand as King Rattler's head came round to see the execution of his new boss; he jerked her on to the floor, falling on top of her to shield her from flying bullets.

And he shouted, 'Wipe 'em out, bounty man! Give 'em hell, cowboy!'

And though his voice was harsh and unmusical there was no mistaking the delight that rang through his words.

As if he'd never liked these people he'd been drinking with, anyway.

Life flooded back to M'Grea with the joy of seeing Bonnie alive and seemingly unhurt. His guns blasted into King Rattler, killing him before he had a chance to kill — killing him even though he was worth two hundred and fifty dollars to him.

But the sheriff didn't surrender. He wasn't the kind to surrender. He was crazy and he went out a crazy way.

He stepped off the balcony and went down shooting his guns empty until a mass of lead suddenly hit him from the rifles below.

Anyway, one way or another, Loco Lou would have had to go out.

Bonnie wasn't in the least hurt, and she made an awful fuss over M'Grea's wounds. Quite openly he said he liked it.

He rose stiffly. She had told him her

story — how a party of Comanches, probably spying on the defeated but still formidable Apaches, had picked her up and taken her to their tepees. How she had been freed to take food just at the moment that the Apache raid had started on the Comanche camp.

In the confusion she had got away on a stray horse; in order to avoid running into any returning Comanche marauders she had ridden down to the Rio Colorado and swum her mount across. She had figured the south bank would be safe from Indians anyway and then a party of Laramie cowboys had stepped out and picked her up.

'They were bargaining with the vigilantes — my life for their freedom — when you came in,' she told him. 'Thank God you did!'

'It was that Easterner who saved your life.'

'Yes.' And she knew about him, too, now. 'He's up here quietly buying up land for a railroad that is projected from Austin. When he told me that I understood a lot.'

'A lot?'

'Yes — why the Laramies by hook or by crook were getting hold of land all along the valley bottom. In some way they'd got to know about the railroad, and they were determined to scoop a fortune out of holding the land when the company needed it for their plans.'

'So you should be a wealthy young lady now, with your bottom-land fetching high railroad prices?'

She nodded, her eyes dancing.

'Does it make any difference?' she whispered.

He looked at her. Nothing made any difference. He slipped his arm round her waist and drawled good-humouredly, 'Guess ef I do have to marry I might as well get me an heiress.' He sighed. 'I don't reckon they'll pay the sher'f of Dead End much, anyway.'

And as he kissed her she realized that the badge that had so recently adorned the shirt of the crazy sheriff of Dead

End was now pinned to his own.

She whispered, 'You'll be a wonderful sheriff, Tom.'

And he was.

We do hope that you have enjoyed reading this large print book.

Did you know that all of our titles are available for purchase?

We publish a wide range of high quality large print books including:
Romances, Mysteries, Classics
General Fiction
Non Fiction and Westerns

Special interest titles available in large print are:
The Little Oxford Dictionary
Music Book, Song Book
Hymn Book, Service Book

Also available from us courtesy of Oxford University Press:
Young Readers' Dictionary
(large print edition)
Young Readers' Thesaurus
(large print edition)

For further information or a free brochure, please contact us at:
Ulverscroft Large Print Books Ltd.,
The Green, Bradgate Road, Anstey,
Leicester, LE7 7FU, England.
Tel: (00 44) **0116 236 4325**
Fax: (00 44) **0116 234 0205**

TWO FROM TEXAS

Neil Hunter

One of the men arrives in Gunner Creek at the end of a long search, whilst the other simply drifts into the town. Fate has drawn them together: two Texans who find a town in trouble — and, being who they were, have to throw in their hands to help. Chet Ballard and Jess McCall are Texicans down to the tips of their boots. Big men with hard fists and fast guns, who see trouble and refuse to back away from it . . .

DERBY JOHN'S ALIBI

Ethan Flagg

Derby John Daggert is out for revenge on his employer after a severe beating meted out for theft and adultery. Then a robbery goes badly wrong, two men are murdered, and the killer makes a wild ride from Querida to Denver. As prime suspect, Daggert is arrested, but his lawyer convinces the jury he was elsewhere when the crime was committed. It is left to Buckskin Joe Swann to hunt down the culprit — a task more difficult than he could have ever imagined . . .

HOOD

Jake Douglas

When he wakes wounded in the badlands, he doesn't even know his own name, where he is, or how he got there. He sure doesn't know who shot him and left him to die. But when the riders come to try and finish the job, they call him 'Hood' . . . Under the scorching sun, he does the only thing he can: straps on a six-gun, gets back in the saddle, and sets out to find out who's on his trail . . .